Coal Miners' Doctor

by
Rita A. Mariotti, M.D.

With sincere appreciation
Rita A Mariotti '93

Bookman Publishing
Martinsville, Indiana

IN MEMORY OF MY SISTER
Dolores Mariotti

ACKNOWLEDGMENTS

The frustrations of writing a book are enlightened only by the support of friends who believed in the project even when the author's enthusiasm waned. For their support and encouragement I want to thank my oldest friends who date back to junior high school: Rita Strassburg, Ann Stumpo and Marian De Rita. For always being there I thank Loris Rosskam and Jean Morris. And for their love and understanding I thank my "junior editors," Brigit Venable and Eleanor Caldwell who made valuable suggestions and corrections while constantly assuring success.

Finally, for her critical comments, rare kudos and pressure to reach my goal I thank my editor, Janice L. Booker. Her questions and comments were the spark that kindled my energy and kept me writing.

My thanks to the editors of *The New York Times, The Philadelphia Inquirer, The Star Ledger, The Pennsylvania Gazette, Now and Then Magazine, and "Transaction & Studies of the College of Physicians"* (forthcoming in the December 2003 issue) for publishing portions of this book in their pages.

INTRODUCTION

When I was a child I wanted to be a nurse. At thirteen I changed my mind. Walking along the grand brownstone mansions on Broad Street in South Philadelphia, I noticed that many of them served as offices and living quarters for prosperous physicians. How elegant and rich these homes appeared to me. Why settle for nursing when I could be a doctor and live in similar grandeur, I thought. Right then I decided that was the life for me. Immediately my aspirations shifted from nursing to medicine. The fact that my family was extremely poor did not seem to matter to me. What teenager analyzes a lifetime decision? It appeared a simple and definitive plan for a student with good grades. My parents and teachers would surely be thrilled with my plan. They were, but with reservations, as they were mature enough to realize that attaining this goal at that time was almost impossible for a female, let alone one with no money.

My teachers kindly but firmly discouraged my ambitions. My parents were supportive and never crushed my aspirations. Years later I learned how they agonized over making my dream a reality. No one in my family had ever been to college. That I could possibly achieve success was extraordinarily impossible for my parents to comprehend.

My mother emigrated from Italy with her parents and an older brother when she was two years old. My grandfather had been offered a job in a construction company run by a prominent Italian-American from the same mountain town of Fornelli, in the Abruzzi section of Italy. The family settled in a three-story home in South Philadelphia, adjacent to the Italian Market on ninth street. My grandparents proceeded over the years to fill the house with ten children, and may have produced more had my mother not taught grandmother about birth control when she herself learned about it in early adulthood. Mother attended the local Catholic school and learned English as well as typical elementary school subjects. She continued classes through the eighth grade when she had to leave to help support the family by working at Wilbur's Chocolate Factory.

Grandmother added cash to the family coffer by renting rooms and serving meals to immigrants settling in the mostly Italian area. About this time a handsome, blonde, blue-eyed musician from Rome roomed at an adjacent home and took his meals at my grandmother's house. When his eyes were not roaming over his flute, he sought pleasure in observing the dark, longhaired, fifteen-year-old beauty, grandmother's oldest daughter. One year later this twenty-two year old musician, Enrico Mariotti, married my mother and moved into her close-knit immigrant family where they eventually raised three children of their own. I was the middle child.

Growing up in an Italian immigrant environment was very protective, probably over protective as I was soon to learn, especially for the young women. I went to South Philadelphia High School for Girls where crossing the corridor to the boys' section was prohibited by school rules. The girls in my family as well as most of my closest friends were not allowed to date, and for many of us our first dating experience with a boy was the high school prom, usually with a cousin or a close friend of the family as our escort, not an encounter for a very romantic affair. I was lucky to have as my date a handsome family friend who lived in Maryland. Although he was somewhat older than I, he readily obliged my family and me by being my escort. I think he felt it would be a fun experience, and because he was one of the few dates who had a car several of our paired classmates were pleased to have him chauffer us to those nightclubs which accepted prom couples. He was the only one old enough to drink beer, which may have been what kept him smiling through the evening. The most awkward moment was when he delivered me home in the early morning hours and

3

stayed overnight on the living room couch as our houseguest.

Our school lives revolved around our close girl-friends. There were no feminists at the time and planning to marry soon after graduation was expected. Going to college was not an easily attainable goal. We were just coming out of the Great Depression, and money was not readily available. My father had long before given up his aspirations for a life as a musician, and after two years of unemployment during the depression he found a fair paying job as a carpenter. The few of us who dreamed about college had to depend upon scholarships for financial assistance. Some of us also had to give up any ideas of marriage. I had a group of eight close friends through junior high and high school, and because we were not allowed to date we called ourselves "The Old Maid's Society." We are still close friends, but only I attained that dreaded eponymous position. All seven of the other women married, although half are now divorced and the rest widowed; only two remain as couples. The freedom from the demands of marriage and parenthood helped me to achieve the goals I set for myself, and I never regretted it.

To become a career woman, much less a physician, was unlikely for young women of my background. Few members of our extended family or their friends ever thought it was possible. I was looked upon as a dreamer, a selfish girl who put her family through financial hardship. I also became a rebel because I left the Catholic Church at age 15 after being sent to sit in a corner and "shut my face" because I asked a nun for an explanation of the Holy Trinity. Surprisingly, my mother supported that decision as much as my decision to become a physician. She stood behind me all my life and had the power and shrewdness to devise plans to make what seemed impossible a reality. Even with her limited education she was comfortable within her person and fit easily into any social situation and made me as proud of her as if she were a college professor. My only embarrassing moment was when she insisted on taking me to college on my first day. She rode the trolley with me to the University of Pennsylvania, deposited me on the steps of the College in my white, flannel, freshman blazer she had made because she could not afford to buy the one the college offered. Just as when she accompanied me to kindergarten, I hid my tears in her warm embrace as she offered me up to a whole new world.

My mother worked out the financial plans for this long-term endeavor by enlisting the cooperation of my older sister and younger brother. My sister worked for an insurance company, and my younger brother was a butcher's apprentice. Their salaries, as well as my father's, were pooled. Mother was the head banker and each week allotted monies wherever needed. There was never obvious dissent because my siblings were not deprived of any real needs.

My father was supportive of everything my mother decided, but she was obviously the family financier and CEO. We were poor, our friends and their families were poor, but none of us ever knew it. The tight family bonds were the most important things that got us through those years. I was able to earn scholarships to college as well as to medical school, but without the family's help those aids would not have been enough. Realistically, I did not know what lay ahead for me in the field of medicine, but it was a dream and a goal that somehow I knew was possible. My family knew even less about what the future would bring, but we planned and worked together until we achieved success.

I did not become the prosperous South Philadelphia physician I fantasized. In the late fifties I interned at Episcopal Hospital in Philadelphia after obtaining my medical degree at The Woman's Medical College of Pennsylvania. I acted the part of a confident intern, self-assured that I knew what was wrong with patients and positive I could cure them. My fellow interns and I shamelessly accepted the adoration and confidence of our poor patients who could not afford their own private physicians. Brilliant diagnoses were made because we had just been graduated from medical school and had memorized what the books had taught us. Horrendous mistakes were made from lack of experience. Basically, we knew nothing about the real world of medicine. During the waning months of internship the sobering reality hit me: I was not ready to go into private practice on my own. I applied to several organizations to do medical missionary work in third world countries, and was rejected because of lack of experience. An advertisement in a medical journal promised experience, adventure, and an attractive stipend of $12,000 a year compared to the annual $1200 earned as an intern. I signed on and entered a very different, unfamiliar universe.

A chain of hospitals owned and operated by the United Mine Workers of America stretched across eastern Kentucky offering free medical care to miners plagued by chronic lung disease. The ad promised pleasant working and living conditions for its medical staff who were culled from all parts of the country. I applied and was accepted. This was a salaried position as a hospital staff member, not an accredited residency program. The position, however, was run much like a residency. Each physician chose the type of specialty he or she preferred, and was supervised by an attending specialist in the field, but no residency credits were given. I chose internal medicine, which was the closest I could get to family practice, my real aspiration.

Practicing in the hills of Kentucky introduced me to unbelievable poverty, and a commitment to patient care that never reaped great financial benefits. Medicine became a passion and a way of life for me that put other desires on hold.

Throughout this book I have changed the names of the counties, cities and other hospitals. The names of all patients as well as doctors have been changed to protect their privacy. I have tried to stick to the facts as I recall them, but it was a long time ago, and I cannot guarantee when past events become blurred by later events in my life. I did not deliberately alter facts for dramatic purposes, but storage areas in the mind can sometimes distort details unintentionally despite all good intentions.

CHAPTER 1

The three story red brick hospital in the little eastern Kentucky town, one-tenth the size of the city hospitals of my training years, was bright and clean against a blue sky, molding itself over the leek-green, tree-covered mountains. In the early morning, fog settled between the mountains like mounds of cotton balls, muffling what few sounds emerged from the small town below. I loved this change from urban life and enjoyed breathing cool air free of industrial fumes.

I stood on the second-floor balcony outside my small efficiency apartment looking apprehensively at the hospital, about one-quarter-city block away from the apartment, separated by a well-kept lawn. To the right of the hospital was an apple orchard surrounding three wooden picnic tables and an outdoor grill. Just beyond, the orchard spread into a wooded area bordering a circuitous stream cutting its way into a small hillside. Surrounding the hospital and apartments were the soft, rolling hills of Kentucky.

Union president John L. Lewis, who held that post from 1920 to 1960, headed the formation of the hospital, one in a chain of eight in Appalachia built by the United Mine Workers of America. The union was notorious for leading a series of strikes that eventually resulted in wage and health improvements for miners. Prior to the militant leadership of Lewis continuing unemployment, extremely dangerous occupational hazards, and company owned towns and stores that drained money and dignity from their workers were the norm in the coal regions of the country. The companies controlled the stores and set prices so workers had no choices. Bills were run up and automatically deducted from the miners' paychecks. Several of these older towns could be seen around eastern Kentucky. The wooden shacks sat side by side in rows going up the hillside. The area was dark and depressing, with poorly built homes immediately adjacent to the mineshafts where everything was covered with coal dust. With union help members got fairer prices and housing improved considerably. With the creation of UMWA Welfare and Retirement Fund miners were assured free hospital and health care for themselves and their families, as well as a pension of $100 a month above age 62. I remember reading about John L. Lewis in the forties and early fifties. I never imagined this short, rotund man with those massive black eyebrows shadowing an angry look would some day be my boss.

I kept looking at the hospital, hesitant to walk over and start this new phase of my life. Suddenly the internship I just left felt more secure, with someone always to lean on for help. Now I was a staff physician, salaried, in authority, and while I yearned for this independence, I was not sure I was ready for it.

I walked with a sense of feigned confidence through the path across the lawn to the entrance of the hospital. As I opened the hospital door my crisp, starched white coat almost wilted from the emerging heat. Hospital odors were subdued by the prevalence of the smell of fresh paint and unused rugs of the newly built hospital. My heart thumped audibly in my inner ear as I looked anxiously into the home of my new medical life. The scraping sound of moving chairs brought to their feet three women scurrying to greet me from the main reception desk just inside the hospital doors. With broad smiles and outstretched hands they welcomed me warmly. Clara, the head receptionist, was the most serious of the three, and her salt and pepper hair added to her mature and authoritative presence. Cindy, a younger assistant receptionist, had a wide, laughing smile and a jovial side waiting to bubble over. Mary, dressed in a white uniform and cap, introduced herself as my nurse. *My nurse!* Suddenly I felt a sense of importance I had never had before. These very friendly women with marked southern accents were greeting me as a superior; someone they looked up to, and were eager to please. As a medical student one feels more like a worm with the surrounding staff a bunch of robins constantly pecking at the student, causing a loss of stature and personality. As an intern you have a false sense of significance fed by an artificial ego, but deep down you know you are the dregs in the barrel about to be washed away. My new assistants suddenly elevated me from vermin-hood, endowing me with a smile as contagious and broad as their own.

The reception area was large and comfortable. At 9 am it was still empty of patients who would soon arrive for appointments with the other staff physicians. Five of us were general practioners and an equal number were specialists in various fields. In addition, visiting specialists, such as pathologists and radiologists, shared duties among several of the other hospitals because they were not large enough for fulltime employment in these more specialized fields. The first floor consisted of the reception area, the emergency room, laboratory, X-ray department, and doctors' offices, all state of the art and well supplied facilities. Mary, my nurse, showed me around the other departments, introducing me as the new physician, then led me down a bright, carpeted corridor leading to my office. I hesitated outside the door, concealing a smile of pleasure as I looked at the newly printed sign, "Rita A. Mariotti, MD." Wouldn't my mother be proud?

I was thrilled with my office. As I entered, colorful geometric patterned curtains softly subdued the brightness of a wall of windows. To my right stood a large desk and swivel chair as well as a consultation chair for the patient. Behind the desk sat a file case upon which rested an X-ray view box. Further back, in front of the windows, was a new examining table, far superior to any I had seen in medical school or internship. A surgical table, bookcases, and sink completed the office accoutrements. A lot of care and professional building technique had gone into furnishing my office as well as the ancillary medical facilities on this first floor of the hospital. I could not help but think that the United Mine Workers of America had taken great pains in spending the union funds with care and purpose. In the ensuing days I would learn the entire hospital was equally well prepared to service the miners with high quality care.

Soon after settling into my office I had a conference with my immediate supervisor, Dr. Ted Joad. He was an internist from the west coast who had relocated with his wife and young son to avoid the hassles and time restrictions of a private practice. He wanted a salaried position with established hours in a small town to afford him more time with his family. Dr. Joad explained my duties and introduced me to the other staff members. He assured me he was available for consultation or discussion of problems any time I needed him. I felt comfortable in his presence and knew I could count on him.

I was quickly assimilated into the hospital routine after making hospital rounds on the patients I inherited from the physician whom I had replaced. I was very pleased with the hospital facilities. One or two bed capacity rooms replaced the large eight to fifteen bed wards of the big city hospitals I was accustomed to in my internship. Patients were comfortable, clean, well fed, and very well cared for by an excellent nursing staff. I could ask for nothing better.

My enthusiasm faltered when I had difficulty bonding with my first patient. Mary Holcomb's 350 pounds weighed heavy on the small hospital bed. The restraining metal side rails pressed against her fleshy arms in an attempt to confine them within the bed limits. She lay flat on her back, snoring heavily around the oxygen and feeding tubes, which filled a mouth and nose whose secretions crusted around the plastic invaders. She had been a resident in these tight quarters for six months since a stroke sent her into comatose vegetation. Three nurses acted as pulleys to shift her immobile layers so that I could examine her lungs and undersurfaces. She frequently lay in watery puddles of excreta, the smell causing our nostrils to twitch and our stomachs to reverse gears. Remarkably, she never developed pneumonia or bed sores. Most of my medical care revolved around balancing her tube feedings to ensure stools that were neither too liquid nor too firm, requiring physical extraction. My inexperience and confusion of my role in this patient's care caused me increasing agitation and dislike of the poor creature. Helpless frustration unfortunately overwhelms logic and humane responses, and daily visits became increasingly more difficult. She was still alive when I left the area two years later.

My reluctant distaste for this patient couldn't match Zeke Bailey's efforts to balance my sentiments. He hated me passionately.

"That damned woman doctor is trying to kill me," he shouted to everyone who would listen.

"She keeps taking my oxygen away. How can I breathe without it?" he lamented.

His lung capacity was limited by fibrosis from chronic black lung disease, the scourge of years of working in the coal mines of eastern Kentucky. My fresh medical training, however, warned that his metabolic condition was being compromised by continuous oxygen flow. I tried to save his life doing what I knew was right, and merely succeeded in losing Zeke to the care of another physician when he insisted I be taken off his case.

Half my day was spent on hospital care of patients, the rest seeing regularly scheduled outpatients in my office. All medical care to miners and their families was free. Emergency room coverage was appointed by one of the staff physicians on a rotating basis. The chronic nature of so many of the hospital-bound patients made the excitement of the emergency room a welcome change. The physicians rotated this service not so much for variety but out of necessity. As the only medical facility in a fifty-mile radius, all medical problems, emergen-

cies, injuries and coal mine disasters became our
venue. It did not take long for me to realize how little medical school had taught me about life and
death and most conditions in between.

Patients from Liggett County were surprised and
hesitant in the presence of a female physician. It
was the first such encounter for most of them. The
quiet, reserved demeanor of these people could be
traced to Welsh and English heritage. Their dialect
was full of Old English idioms, which added a
Chaucerian flavor. One of our physicians was later
to trace and document much of the phraseology to
Chaucer's writings. It was not because these people
read such literature, but rather their closeness and
inbreeding kept the language traits passing down
from one generation to another.

The first patient to arrive on my emergency
service was a man covered with a thick layer of coal
dust, making the whites of his eyes and teeth prominent. We got used to miners leaving a residue of
black powder on seats when they stood. There was
always fallout on your hand after a welcoming
handshake. I never understood, however, how a
miner arrived for a morning appointment still covered with coal dust after a night's sleep. What did
his wife and his bed sheets look like when he got out
of bed? At this time, my black powdered friend quietly informed me a copperhead snake had bitten
him. The beating of my heart echoed through the
empty memory chambers of my brain. Who ever

treated snakebite in Philadelphia? Fortunately, both patient and nurse were skilled in such treatment. When bitten, the miner had placed a tourniquet around his lower leg and suctioned the wound. My efficient nurse led me to the snake venom antiserum assuring me a successful cure was available for this common emergency.

In the adjoining room a pale, thin girl lay on the gurney. She appeared much younger than the twelve years registered on the chart. Her mother wore the typical look of a miner's wife. Non-smiling, thin, faded lips pressed worry lines deep into her colorless cheeks. Expressionless eyes stared from under straight prematurely graying hair. Two smaller children wiped their noses on shabby frayed coat sleeves as they hung on to her loose-fitting black and white checkered dress. The mother's tender caress as she stroked the sick child's face belied her outward appearance of distance.

Peggy's eyes sunk into her sick face. She suddenly elevated her head from the stretcher. Her arm groped the air in an agitated, pleading way. The attentive nurse produced an emesis basin when she understood the reason for the child's flapping arm, too late for the projectile tide of vomit that missed the basin. Floating in this bilious mess were three large, fat, roundworms. Slithering toward me, the six by one-half inch creatures caused me to visibly draw back and cowardly run from the emergency room. When the nurse got everything cleaned she ushered me back into the room quietly suggesting we proceed with arrangements to admit the child. Peggy was well known to the emergency room staff. She and her family had been treated numerous times for recurrent Ascaris worm infestations. Her case, however, had been resistant to treatment and she gradually worsened. She was admitted to the hospital and in a few days would become comatose as the worms entered her central nervous system.

It was not difficult to understand why worms were such a problem in eastern Kentucky. Patients lived in one or two room shacks frequently housing six to eight children plus parents. An outhouse was some distance away and it was not unusual for the children to defecate around the house rather than walk the distance. Winter or summer the children were barefooted. Refuse was carried in and about the house. With no running water, hand washing was not readily available. The lack of cleanliness ensured constant reproduction of worm ova carried by the oral fecal route.

That evening I walked across the hospital grounds toward my apartment, wanting to put the events of the day behind me. The cool October breeze was refreshing. The tree in front of the apartment complex adjoining the hospital had a few remaining apples hanging heavily on tired branches. I picked a nice red one, bit into it, and a tiny white worm wiggled a defiant dance.

CHAPTER 2

Living alone was a joy. I had been raised in a row home in South Philadelphia sharing a bedroom with my older sister. My younger brother kept diminishing the already cramped quarters of our home by introducing a variety of homeless pets, and my sister was not happy with our living arrangements when she had to make room for the embalmed cat I frequently brought home from my college course in Cat Anatomy. I could not understand why this upset her. Wasn't the larger burden on me? I had to listen to endless hours of Frank Sinatra music. Her nightly routine of clicking large curlers over her hair, polishing her nails, and sucking long and hard through a straw for the last bubbles of Coke irritated me.

My furnished efficiency apartment was one of twenty built by the United Mine Workers of America to house the incoming staff of doctors and nurses. Ten adjacent apartments on the top floor and an equal number below were reached by outside metal corridors similar to low cost motels blossoming throughout the nation. It was difficult to sneak in without being heard as well as a struggle not to hear your neighbors' activities through the thin walls. The windows looked toward the grounds and creek behind the hospital and beyond to the mountains. On one of my days off, I prepared myself for an afternoon of complete relaxation. I felt so antebellum, sipping Southern Comfort on the rocks, as I shook my feet out of hospital shoes and into warm socks. I lit up a cigarette and felt a slight burning in my stomach along with a sense of nausea, which caused an involuntary frown. I was always on some diet or other, and the lack of food, coupled with smoking and the drink, caused this unpleasant sensation. The newspaper lay scattered around my big easy chair and on the footstool propping my wool encased feet. As usual, my toes were cold, and the frequent wiggling of my feet to warm them resulted in the rustling of papers. The roaring of the wind was suddenly louder as it whistled through the partially opened window. I arose to close it, and looked out over the countryside. It was the first snow of the year. The mountains, with their clinging cluster of small homes, were transformed into lovely patterns of white patches among graceful black shadows. The natives described the wintry mountains as "bleak, depressing, and lonely." To me they were as beautiful as they had been in the fall, covered by the splendor of their multicolored coat. Once the leaves were shed the mountains achieved a new character and mystery that had been lost in full dress. Curves and contours appeared which curtains of foliage had previously hidden. The grandeur of my surroundings never failed to soothe me, probably because they were in sharp contrast to the limited view from my South Philadelphia home. In Kentucky I could see a sunset blazing gloriously across the entire sky. In Philadelphia the sun could only be seen for brief moments because the sky was obscured by endless rows of tiny homes on our small street.

My apartment was warm and cozy. It was untidy, as usual, but it had that lived in flavor. The books were neatly stacked on top of the desk. A cuddly stuffed puppy nestled against the books, looking happy and content. For a stuffed music box he certainly had a lot of personality. It brought back memories of a happy internship, and of the grateful patient who had presented him to me as a gift. There were so many times, especially early in my practice of medicine, that I was plagued with insecurities in patient care. Then there were times when a patient gave you total credit for saving his or her life. It was most likely a team effort, but it felt good to think all my training really reaped success and perhaps I did save her life. Moments of patient gratitude caused a warm glow in me and a sense of achievement that cannot help but boost an ego shrouded by doubts.

As I looked around the apartment I was glad the furniture was light pine because it hid accumulated dust. The two convertible bed-sofas against the walls were neat except for the night pillow and extra

blanket, which were kept ready for a possible
Sunday afternoon nap. I never tired of looking at
the scroll my Japanese high school pen pal had sent
me which was hanging against the Wedgwood blue
wall. It blended well with the huge world map
adorning the contrasting pale yellow wall. The map
had colored pushpins scattered about it where fantasy trips were planned to satisfy my lifelong desire to
travel the world. Between the beds was a large
table, perfect to use as a work area for the model
ship I was building. But there it lay, the carved
unfinished hull nicely mounted and awaiting com-
pletion.

I had only been in the apartment a few months,
but I had many projects going at the same time and
not enough room to house them all. I was also in the
process of building a radio-phonograph from a kit.
Building a stereo unit was popular in the late fifties
thanks to Heath Kit units, which supplied full parts
and instructions. All I needed was time and quiet
and living alone provided this. There was far more
free time in this practice than I ever had during medical school or internship. All patient visits were by
appointment, there were no house calls, hospital
rounds were completed in the mornings, and emergency room call duties were on prescheduled days.
Most weekends were free, and the extra time offered
me so many options I had difficulty with selections.
I ended up involved in so many different projects I
could not complete one before becoming interested

in yet another.

The dining area of the apartment was on one side of my combined living room-bedroom. It consisted of only a table and two chairs, but the drop-leaf table afforded me more working space. At the entrance of the apartment was a Pullman type kitchen adjacent to the one room efficiency. A small corridor opposite the kitchen was furnished as a dressing room with closets and a chest of drawers, and next to it, completing the quarters, was a small bathroom.

I learned to enjoy privacy and isolation without ever feeling lonely. My tiny kitchen offered me new experiences into the joy of cooking. One is not raised in an Italian family without appreciating a love for food and wine. Fine eating was part of my heritage. Discovering how to produce it on my own became a passion.

When I first arrived in Kentucky, my new wealth made me want to accumulate even more. I started learning how to cook economically. One of my favorite creations was a stew made from browned chicken necks, wings, and backs, simmered with fresh carrots, celery and onions. Perked by wine and herbs and served over steamed rice this concoction became an elegant meal, especially when accompanied by recently discovered Rhine wine. I enjoy it to this day although I have never served it to guests. How many of my sophisticated friends in my retirement years would really enjoy a meal made from such humble chicken parts?

As my acquaintances at the hospital grew, my cooking skills reached higher levels as I ventured to entertain them. As a child of Italian immigrants, I knew cranberry sauce as a disgusting dusky rose-colored gel that slid from a can and sat limply next to otherwise exciting turkey accoutrements. In Kentucky I learned cranberries were real, bright red, beautiful berries that cooked into a grandiose brilliant ruby-studded mixture as far from the cranberry sauce of my youth as was a truffle from a turnip.

Pizza was unknown in Appalachia. I decided to introduce it. I made the dough from flour, water and yeast. The standard toppings of tomato, olive oil, garlic, oregano, and mozzarella cheese melted sensuously over the homemade, brown crust. The unfamiliar smell seeped through the windows and doors and, like the Pied Piper, drew an assortment of curious and hungry neighbors more than willing to experiment with a food that produced such an enticing aroma.

I enjoyed cooking my own meals, but many of the other tenants preferred eating at the hospital cafeteria because it was easier. The meals were not part of our salary as they were during internship, but they were inexpensive and typical of bland, boring hospital fare. I chose to limit myself to coffee during mid-morning breaks because I was not to be trusted in front of a cafeteria line overflowing with calorific choices. The leaner members of the hospital staff enjoyed a sweet for a perk up. Married male physicians who lived in nearby rented homes ate lunch at the hospital but had their main evening meal with their families. Food was not a passionate subject, and dining out a rarity. There was a small sandwich shop in the town center, but there were no restaurants nearby. If a group of us decided to eat out it was usually on a Sunday when we would drive an hour or two to find a suitable place, usually connected to a small hotel. When we could get away for several days we drove to State Parks which had lodges and more adequate dining facilities.

The only memorable eating experiences I had in Kentucky were when I was fortunate to be invited to a patient's home, or to the homes of our Appalachian staff members. There were no true gourmets among my physician acquaintances, and a simple fare of steak and chops was the norm.

I learned to eat unusual and sometimes eccentric foods at the home of my friends who lived in the area. Sam Holcomb, a male nurse from Harlan, Kentucky, had so enjoyed his first experience with my pizza he invited me home to sample his special dish. He refused to tell me more because he wanted it to be a complete surprise.

Sam and his wife, Polly, greeted me at their home with cordial enthusiasm. Any other people I have known around the world have never surpassed the sincerity and friendship the people of eastern Kentucky showed toward the invading foreigners.

Whether professionals, businessmen, miners, or long-term welfare recipients, their modest homes were offered as gracious palaces for the comfort and pleasure of their guests. I accepted their hospitality humbly and always felt regally treated.

Home brewed beer was the harbinger of local entertainment. A frothy, heady start it was. One taste and an enduring love affair for malt ensued. I brew small caldrons to this day, but selfishly hoard the distillation in my private stash. It never tastes the same as its Kentucky ancestor. The flavors added by the huge outside stills and lack of sterility is missing. The excitement of hiding from government revenuers imbued a savored joy that legal beers lack. Fortunately, I never developed a taste for illegal home distilled spirits or White Lightning, a vile and dangerous concoction reserved for serious local consumption. A sip burned the pillars of the tongue, singed the esophagus, and came to a final resting place in a liver whose cells gave up their lives for the owner's drunken pleasures.

I was on my third beer when Polly proudly brought her favorite dish to the table. On the floating tails of steam rising from the country crock an enticing, hearty odor flowed by my nostrils, stimulating gastric juices. A hunter's stew of muskrat, raccoon, and squirrel would normally have shaken me. Dishes using these animal ingredients did not exist in any of my recipe files. The appetizing odors, however, mixed with the softening effects of the beer, made the meal more than memorable. I was happily bread mopping the remaining sauce when Sam proudly presented me with the special treat. Because I was the guest of honor, the squirrel's skull was saved and offered to me to suck out what was considered the best part of the meal: the squirrel's brains. I could not do it. I could not raise this tiny white head to my lips and suck the contents through the eye socket. In an eternal second my mental computers analyzed all acceptable and courteous denials. They all failed, and the shame of my reaction caused me great discomfort. I reminded myself of Italian foods where I ingested blood pudding, chicken intestines, calf hearts and lungs, and even sucked meat from bones of chicken feet. Was this so much worse? Yes. That skull was so tiny and rodent-like it caused me to squirm visibly. I very apologetically looked up from my plate and said to my hosts,

"I am so sorry, I just cannot do this. The food was so great, but this looks too much like a rat's head."

Sam's response was a hearty laugh uplifting my rejection with charm.

"Forgive me, Rita, I wasn't thinking. I should have realized this might be too foreign an experience for you. Our other friends always fight over who should get the skull because the contents are so sweet, and I wanted you to have the same pleasure. Don't worry about it; I am just glad you enjoyed the rest of the meal so much."

As I left their home I was graciously invited back with the promise that the next meal would not include such vivid anatomical parts, and we all enjoyed a parting laugh. When I returned to my apartment and replayed the events of my visit, I became annoyed at my reactions. I should have tried the delicacy. Was sucking on the lower end of a chicken's sacrum so different from sipping on a squirrel's brains? When I told other people about my experience I learned I had indeed missed out on an exceptional taste, but I never again sought to become an aficionado of squirrel brains and put the matter behind me.

The staff apartments surrounded the hospital. The closeness of our quarters wove a net binding our lives like a spider controlling its captives. The normal quiet of my apartment was disturbed by sounds beyond my neighbor's wall. I wanted to play records to muffle the sounds, but I had not yet completed the building of my stereo set, so I tried to read or ignore what was happening next door.

John West, my good neighbor, was retired from general practice in Lexington, Kentucky, and he had decided to spend a year in the Miners' Hospital before he and his wife planned to travel the country in a motor home. She lived in Lexington, and he spent his weekends at their home. During the week he was my quiet neighbor except for the nights he entertained his girlfriend. John wore his age of sixty-two well. Short, rotund, and bald, he spent an inordinate amount of time cupping his hands around his pipe and lighting it to keep the noisome dottle alive. His wire-framed glasses magnified the twinkle in his eyes and his slow, grunting spurts of laughter made his company a pleasure. But a romantic figure he was not. Helena, an unmarried hospital secretary in her thirties, must have found him just that. She spent at least three nights a week with him.

I was not bothered by their affair, happy they enjoyed each other. However, John's bed was separated from mine only by thin plaster wallboard. During their lovemaking I confined myself to the other side of my room, trying to keep busy with more unromantic matters. When their activities stilled, and I envisioned a short pipe lighting ceremony finalizing the act, I climbed quietly on my side of our split sleeping accommodations. I usually read myself to sleep and our neighborly arrangements worked well. A problem arose when the occasional middle of the night erection stimulated further activity. The duplicate bed creaked and shook, and the occupants moaned and groaned in my ear. The pillow folded over my head helped subdue the sounds, but the vibrating wall and remembering the lover of my internship year contributed to my involuntary grand mal orgasm.

CHAPTER 3

Nothing as exotic as squirrel brains ever appeared in our hospital kitchen, for which I was grateful. The kitchen became a place where the pleasantries of foods, intertwined and seasoned by the presence of a variety of people, produced an interesting pastiche.

I spent several late evenings a week in the hospital kitchen. Trying to keep within an eight-dollar a week food budget often made me hungry before bedtime. It wasn't as if I could drive to town for fast food. The closest shop to buy an ice cream cone was eight miles away and the nearest *McDonald's* was fifty miles from the hospital. *McDonald's Hamburger* was just starting to open its chain in the fifties and how I later wished I had invested with them.

The basement kitchen was where the local hospital employees gathered when the shift changed. It was a time to loosen up, share the day's gossip and plan future activities. They knew each other well and unlike being with a group of physicians there were no egos to contend with.

Billy Joe was always the first to show for the

late evening snack. I remember him so well. His
6'3" frame was held together by an impressive
amount of soft fat flesh that flowed to the paunch
protruding over his well-worn belt. His large,
bumpy nose dominated a sharply carved face. His
eyes were small with wrinkle lines at the corners
that seemed raised in an accessory smile comple-
menting the wide grin that appeared when Millie
was conducting food preparations. Billy Joe was
the night custodian who needed nourishment to continue working his late night hours. His wife had
died four years earlier, and Millie, night chef and
kitchen manager, sustained both his physical and
emotional needs.

Millie had a rare quality of bringing laughter to
any situation. She saw humor in everything, and
told stories that wrung laughter from even hardened
pessimists. All hospital gossip was replayed in
Millie's kitchen as comedy. She did not tell foolish
jokes but rather played life as if it were one comic
tale after another. Everyone enjoyed listening to her
and the laughter was contagious. A neat, attractive
woman in her late forties, she had a young, rosy
complexion, and an ample bosom that moved in
rhythm with her giggling laughter.

Whenever more than four people gathered, a
guitar was sure to appear. Billy Joe played his every
night. He stood with one foot on a chair and
strummed away with the ease and simplicity of a
natural and seasoned player. I was thrilled by these

performances, and vowed to take guitar lessons. On one of my trips back home I bought a fifty dollar Gibson guitar and five self-instruction learning books. I studied night after night playing *On Top of Old Smokey,* and *Red River Valley* over and over again. I never did have an ear for music, as my father would attest from failed efforts to teach me to play the piano. Daddy, who was an accomplished flutist and a child musical prodigy in Italy, was sure I was tone deaf. Well, I kept playing the guitar on and off for fifteen years and never progressed beyond the first of the five self-teaching books I had purchased. Billy Joe tried to help me in my endeavor to coax music out of my guitar, but he learned early on it was a hopeless task. I finally sold the Gibson thirty-five years later as a practically unused antique for three hundred dollars. The handsome $250 profit never made up for my miserable failure as a musician.

The kitchen staff was at first amused and surprised by my visits. Some of the nurses, but none of the other doctors, had ever joined their circle. Of the five general practitioners I was the only one who was single and lived alone. There was one other woman physician living on the premises when I first arrived, but she lived with her husband. The three other physicians were married men who were comfortably settled at home with their families in the evenings. The attending specialists all lived in residences short distances from the hospital and had no reason to spend time in the hospital kitchen late at night. On the rare occasions I felt a little home sick, the feeling was quickly dispelled when I joined the kitchen gatherings. I enjoyed socializing with the locals. I felt like one of the gang and was easily included by them, accepted as a friend rather than a physician, but always referred to as "doctor," or "Doc," which I acknowledged as their form of respect. I have always felt that patients exhibit a sense of awe when confronted with physicians on a social level. They will remain somewhat uncomfortable until they discover the doctor's ease in their presence. I believe it is easier for a female physician to achieve a personal bond; perhaps it's that umbilical tie. On the other hand, I have been somewhat offended over the years when workmen refused to give me the same respect they gave my male colleagues. Whenever I contracted workers they always called me by my first name even when I referred to them as "Mister," while they kept referring to male physicians as "Doctor" so and so.

It was fun to listen to local gossip told in Appalachian patois and with country flare. My personal speech was quickly infiltrated with Appalachian mannerisms as my family and friends noted on my visits home. "I reckon you're right," or "that whiskey will heat you plumb up," or "I declare, you sure are funny," or "I hollered right loud," were some of the expressions that slipped out when I was "up north."

When the shift changed, the outgoing staff headed for home and the incoming shift of workers replaced them in their various hospital positions. Millie and I were left alone, she to her kitchen tasks and I to listen to her endless tales. I learned a lot about Millie in those late night sessions. I realized years later these talks were the beginning of my psychotherapy training sessions. Millie needed to talk and I needed to listen and to analyze, but rarely offered advice.

Millie had married at age 16, and suffered through unhappy years with a husband who spent half of his life in the coalmines, resulting in a lifelong struggle with black lung disease. The other half of his life was consumed deep in the "hollers." The hills of eastern Kentucky roll endlessly and cut deep crevices in the land. They sink into the flatlands on one side and rise upward and backward, creating hollow formations, deeply set valleys between the mountains. It is in these "hollers," as everyone called them, that the miners built their homes for protection from the cold, the elements, and from invading strangers. Snow formed in the mountain cavities and when spring came the thaw provided adequate water supplies for homes with no running water. Central heating was limited to one wood stove per house. Most homes were one-room wooden shacks housing six to eight children. Gardening was terraced up the sides of the mountain. It did not seem to hurt the quality of the "roasting ears" or the "shucky beans," staple crops of the area. Sweet corn was grown to roast over outdoor fires, locking in memorable flavors. Green beans were planted and left on the vines long past the time one would normally pick them to eat as tender young beans. They stayed on the vines until they were long, thick, hard and devoid of any green coloration. The resulting orange-brown-speckled monster-sized shells were then picked and literally strung across the wooden porches. Each pod was pierced by needle and thread and linked together. They danced in the wind like voodoo dolls until the beans, colliding against the dry shell, rattled a tune announcing the proper level of dryness. At that point they became "shucky beans." As each bean was hand shucked out of the dry shell it fell into a pan as a group of shiny, speckled, irregularly shaped marbles. Floating in a pot of water awash with greasy chunks of salt-pork and fresh mustard greens, the beans reached a cholesterol busting height of savory excellence.

High into the "hollers" another hidden industry flourished: moonshine. The hollows between the mountains were great places to hide stills from the government revenuers. Moonshine was a thriving business. With so many people out of work, where the money surfaced to finance the habit was puzzling.

I learned from Millie that her husband, Jason, ran a successful still at the base of Lonesome Hill.

His White Lightning brought a good price, but Millie never saw much of the profits. Jason imbibed a large portion of the liquor, producing a continuous state of drunken stupor. Black lung disease, (anthracosis or scarring of lung tissue by coal dust) coupled with damage to the liver by the poisonous effect of the illegal grain distillation, White Lightning, staged a shortened life span for Jason. Millie was left with three children to rear on her own. They lived on welfare for many years, as did a large number of the miners' families when the mines closed. Millie's life and that of many others in Appalachia greatly improved when jobs became available with the opening of the chain of Miners' Hospitals.

Despite her hard life with Jason, Millie spoke fondly of him. In her inimitable way she described their lovemaking sessions vividly, almost too vividly for me. She laughingly portrayed sexual positions and body contortions I knew only from purloined glances at the *Kama Sutra* I found hidden in the stacks of the college library when a student. My innocent smile only pressed her into more intimate details. That was the first of many subsequent experiences of ignorance of sex that made me wish a course in sexual education had been offered in medical school. It was shocking that Luci Arnez of the *I Love Lucy* series could not use the word "pregnancy" in her televised show in the fifties. It was more shocking that medical students were sheltered from a sexual education during the same era. No wonder patients were uncomfortable discussing sex with doctors who were just as uncomfortable listening to them let alone trying to offer advice.

With the openness of the sixties, medical schools changed their tune about sex education. I recall speaking to younger women physicians as they started infiltrating the suburbs of New Jersey where I had ranked as the only practicing female for several years. They were far more knowledgeable about sex than I had ever been at their age. Perhaps it was from personal experience during the liberal sixties with the flourishing commune culture, or maybe medical schools had finally incorporated sex education programs. I leaned more toward the former choice. While my patients considered me a mature, learned, matriarchal person, my younger female colleagues often saw me as a maiden aunt figure. It wasn't until a few years before retirement that I earned the status of a pioneer in the evolving struggle of women physicians to gain respect in South Jersey.

During my early years of practice I was always uneasy discussing sex with patients. One patient complained she wanted children, but admitted that in ten years of marriage she had never had sex because she was afraid of intercourse and the pain it caused. I tried to teach her how to stretch her imperforate hymen when I should have insisted she be immediately hospitalized for surgical correction. I had my male colleagues to thank for helping me out of some ignorant spots, and later my own personal sexual experiences to use as guidelines. My closest associate always answered my naïve questions about sex with kindness, but years later we both laughed at how ridiculous I had sounded. With the passage of years I was to become the Dr. Ruth of my generation. My male patients discussed their most intimate sexual problems with me, confiding also their out of wedlock acts of prowess. Women sought my advice on abortions as well as same sex relationships. Homosexual males found me more compassionate than male physicians who were uncomfortable discussing gay sexual problems. Homosexual females made me apprehensive at first, especially when they eyed me with a questioning glance. I gained their confidence when we both relaxed and accepted each other's sexual prefer-ences with respect. I gave a series of community lectures on female sexuality, which were generally well accepted, except by one married woman with two children who bragged that her husband of thirty years had never seen her nude. She walked out of my lecture in disgust when I tried to teach the women how to incorporate masturbation into some sexual performances.

Millie, fortunately, never asked my advice about her love life. While she flaunted her sexual experi-ences with Jason she never divulged her relationship with Billy Joe. Their intimacy was well known and accepted by hospital personnel, but was not a subject for discussion. Both of them remained my closest non-medical friends throughout my time in eastern Kentucky.

In one of my kitchen sessions I asked Billy Joe whether he performed his music professionally. He admitted to playing the guitar at various social events about town, especially at square dances. I learned how to square dance in college, but had never attended a real country affair. I asked Billy Joe what he thought about joining me in organizing an evening social right on the hospital grounds. I had been on the staff several months and, while I knew almost everyone in the hospital, we had not joined together as a social group. In medical school and internship the medical personnel frequently met for social gatherings, but because of the hospital size these events were limited to doctors and nurses only. With the compactness of the Miners' Hospital we had a great opportunity to throw a party where all the hospital employees and the medical staff could meet and enjoy each other's company. Up to this point the doctors had entertained one another at their respective homes once or twice, but nothing on a scale as large as Billy Joe and I were planning. We decided between us that we would have a square dance right on the hospital grounds. I would seek permission from the Chief of Staff and the hospital administrator. Funding for food would be provided by the administration, or if necessary by contributions from the medical staff itself. Billy Joe would round up local talent to provide the necessary dance caller as well as guitar and banjo players. He was pleased with the idea, as were several other hospital employees who were listening in on our plans.

When I presented my ideas to the hospital administrator he was very much in favor of a party involving the entire hospital personnel and medical staff. He, the kitchen staff, and Billy Joe did most of the work arranging for the event. I sought the support of the medical staff. At first they showed little enthusiasm, but as the time for the square dance approached their interest grew. I was reminded of the "International Night Party" I had promoted during internship. We had a multinational group of interns and residents at Episcopal Hospital in Philadelphia including Indians, Egyptians, Iranians, Africans, and Filipinos. I thought we could get each ethnic group to plan a cultural skit in native costume to perform a dance, song, play an instrument, or tell jokes. The American staff members could do a skit of their own, or join one of the other groups. I chose to join with my roommate, Nebbie, and her family and African friends from Ghana. I was in love with her brother-in-law, Joe, and found this was a way to get closer to him. We dressed in native costumes, spent time rehearsing with her musician husband, and eventually danced across the stage like pros. The rehearsals and the performance did much to bring Joe and I even closer. The event was a huge success, and I yearned for a repeat outcome for the square dance affair.

The medical staff at Miners' Hospital was not as ethnically diversified and tended more toward elitism. With my upbringing as an Italian-American I personally felt more comfortable with the Appalachians than the upper-middle class physicians. I had struggled during my early years of schooling feeling like an outsider and foreigner because my parents and grandparents were immigrants. While they sought to attain citizenship, they encouraged us to learn English and avoid speaking Italian to them. During the forties we were so into Americanism that we fought hard to lose our Italian image. It was a wrong decision, and I have long regretted it as well as the opportunity to be able to learn Italian as a second language. The older I got the more proud of my Italian heritage I became, and the more I regretted being embarrassed by it as a teenager. Class distinctions were a reality in high school. I felt inferior to my instructors and resented them even when I knew my own sensitivities were at fault. When I was turned down for a senatorial scholarship in South Philadelphia I blamed it on my ethnic status. I was less aware of class separateness in college. It was probably there, but I was so busy working for good grades to maintain the scholarship the University of Pennsylvania had granted me and to work toward getting into medical school that I was aware of little else.

In the medical field there were definite class barriers. The chief of staff was a class higher than the surgeon, and he a class above the internist, and so on down the scale to the general practitioner. This did not bother me as much as the wives of the physicians who placed themselves equally in this artificial ranking of superiority. The trim, elegant, diamond studded wife of the surgical chief in my New Jersey hospital, voiced openly that any woman wearing over a size six was a pig. She rarely associated with the wife of the family physician. I, the lone and unmarried female physician, was a dilemma to the doctor's wives. Was I to be categorized as a physician or a woman competing with the wives for a top spot in the hierarchy of social elevation? I made it easy for them when I refused to join the hospital Women's Auxiliary and remained a member of the hospital staff as just one of the guys.

The medical staff at Miners' was less concerned with status but they did keep within their social levels. They were far more likely to socialize with local legal and newspaper professionals than the hospital personnel or their patients. Billy Joe was the first to question whether the doctors would really join in dancing with the locals, but I assured him it would not be a problem.

And, indeed, it was not. When the big night arrived everyone showed up for the fete. The local personnel got the performance off and running smoothly by swinging and twirling their colorfully dressed ladies with rhythmic charm and precision.

It was my job to prod the stiff, uncoordinated city doctors, and make them shed their stilted persona so they would dance comfortably with the locals. It wasn't long before they began to smile and then laugh, enjoying the festivities. By evening's end hospital visitors and even ambulatory patients joined in the revelry. The music and camaraderie captivated everyone, resulting in a fun-filled homogenized blend.

CHAPTER 4

The telephone became a hated instrument, especially when rattling me from a deep and welcome sleep. I spent hours conniving how to keep nurses' home phones ringing all night after they woke me repeatedly requesting sleeping pills for insomniac patients. When my phone rang for a bonafide emergency, there was no time to think as I threw myself into hospital clothes and ran the short distance across the grounds to the emergency room.

On one occasion, when I arrived breathless in the emergency room, Jesse Campbell lay quietly on the E.R. bed clutching his chest. His wide eyes spoke the fear that his tongue could not express. His vital signs were stable and the injected morphine produced almost instant relief of his chest pain. His eyelids relaxed and covered soft brown eyes. After blood was drawn for analysis, the intravenous fluid ran through the needle keeping an open pathway; oxygen flowed via a nasal catheter. We moved him on his bed to a small private room to do an electrocardiogram. There were no monitoring screens, no elaborate electrical connections, no rush of nurses or other staff members, and no code blue. The scene

consisted of the patient, doctor, one nurse, intravenous tube, nasal oxygen, and morphine. This was
1959 in an isolated hospital in the hills of depressed
Appalachia. The electrocardiogram confirmed a
heart attack and heparin, a blood thinner, was added
to the treatment.

Jesse's wife had the same lack of expression typical of miners' wives. She did, however, appear to
be relieved when I told her Jesse was resting comfortably and that everything we could do was being
done. Mrs. Campbell returned to the waiting room
and I settled down to a long night of observation. I
kept seeing Jesse's anxious eyes; their sense of fear
and danger was contagious.

The stillness of the room was interrupted by a
groan. The whites of Jesse's eyes rolled to promi-
nence as his breath stopped. The stethoscope heard
only my own heart thumping in my ears. He had no
peripheral pulses, his pupils, high in their sockets,
were dilated. His face and hair was slick with
sweat. THWACK! My fist hit his chest – once –
twice. Nothing. My mouth girded his as I blew hot,
nervous breath into his lungs. THWACK! – Again.
Nothing. As I screamed for the nurse I found the
vial of adrenalin on the emergency cart and drew up
the standard amount into a syringe fitted with a four-
inch cardiac needle. My fingers slid over his left
fifth anterior rib on to the soft space above. With the
needle poised I entered the skin and muscle, and
pushed into more resistant cardiac musculature.

When blood swirled up into the syringe I plunged the fluid into the left ventricle, withdrew the needle, and released my breath. My hand resting on his chest felt his heart and mine beating as one. The nurse was there in an instant and we both were encouraged by the return of a few heartbeats. They did not last. The quivering fibrillation of a dying heart refused to reverse. It was 1959; electro-cardio version, stimulation of the heart by hand held electric paddles to convert to normal rhythm, had not yet been invented. There was nothing more I could do. Jesse died.

The sense of hopelessness and despondency over the loss of a patient never changes, even after forty years of practicing medicine. Feelings of inadequacy and anger plague you. Could something else have been done? Could the death have been prevented? With a mind twisted by doubts, the body somehow finds the courage to inform the family and give needed support. Death is the single most difficult crisis a physician must face, and it never gets easier.

I walked the hospital floors while the body traveled to the morgue. The quiet of the night was interrupted by an occasional distant snore, and the sound of a nurse's heels receding along shining linoleum corridors. As I passed Jesse's room a small light reflected over the crumpled sheets on his empty bed. I stared, haunted by the memory of fear in his eyes. I realized then that he knew he was going to die.

Tomorrow I would complain to my colleagues about losing sleep and spending an unsuccessful night on call. We frequently joked and made accusations to hide the hurt felt after losing a patient. Tonight, however, I walked to the bed, lay on the sheets still moist from Jesse's sweat, and wept.

CHAPTER 5

With little to do in the surrounding area of the hospital it was common for the occupants of the apartments to entertain each other frequently. At least once a week someone threw a party. Picnic tables and an outdoor grill on the side of the hospital, away from patient rooms, offered opportunities for informal entertaining. This large grassy area sat next to a refreshing stream that invited long walks by its banks, provided strollers did not mind the occasional copperhead snake that surfaced to sun itself. We sat on the lawn eating and drinking, and momentarily forgot our other life that existed within the hospital walls.

The owners of the local grocery store delighted in our cookouts. They sold more expensive steaks to the doctors for one party than they sold to miners' families in an entire year. Our medical staff had an increase in female physicians after I arrived. Raquel Conn and I were the first to be employed. When our fellow classmates, also trying to find their way in the new world of medicine, heard how much we were enjoying our positions, two others signed on. Hideko Yoshino was to replace Raquel when her husband insisted they move on to the more cultured life of Los Angeles. Hideko became the new OB-GYN resident, and Joan Ebert signed on as pathologist just before I left after two years. A female pediatrician from the south joined the staff early on, but male physicians were still in the majority. Our parties on the lawn and in the apartments were a mixture of both male and female medical staff, as well as nursing and laboratory personnel. Frequently physicians from neighboring Miners' Hospitals joined the festivities.

Our Japanese-American resident, Hideko, supplied us with Rhine wine that she had shipped in by the case from California. It was a crisp, dry wine – so different from the homemade, bold, purple-red wines that leaped from the cantinas of the rowhomes in South Philadelphia. I could imagine my grandfather's jaws tightening so as to make his lips frown if he would sniff this pale, white wine. To drink it with red meat would be anathema and make him shudder visibly! To me, however, it was a new, fresh taste, and an experience I enjoyed thoroughly.

I had not learned many formal social skills at this time of my life, but after accepting so many invitations even I knew it was probably time I reciprocated with a party of my own. I chose to entertain in my apartment because I felt more comfortable cooking pasta (and, of course, it was cheaper.)

The dinner started with an antipasto no Italian would recognize. The unavailable ingredients of imported prosciutto and soprassata (special Italian salami) were replaced with boiled ham and Lebanon salami. Vinegar preserved cherry peppers became local hot chilies, and dry, cardboard-like American processed cheese substituted for sharp Italian provolone. The saddest substitution was canned olives for dried, oil-cured black olives. Nevertheless, when local grown lettuce leaves were added it turned into a colorful and acceptable substitute for the real thing. The pasta course was a garlic-oil based sauce with crisp bacon pieces substituting for fresh Pancetta. Frozen green peas and mixed dried herbs added color and taste while goat cheese was a surrogate for imported Parmesan. This strange but interesting change made for a surprisingly tasty pasta dish. A good red wine had taken me a twenty-five mile trip to find its way to the table, but it was worth it. My grandmother's classic recipe for pound cake, accompanied by fresh fruit, made a nice end to a simple Italian meal, which seemed to appeal to the culturally diverse group.

My dinner party was a success. A large quantity of food and wine had been consumed with everyone entering into free and happy conversation. Finally, the wine took its toll and my guests stole out one by one. As the wine dominated my cerebral cells I felt the need to lie down and close my eyes. Everyone had left except for two women who sat and talked quietly near my sated body. I seemed asleep, breathing deep, alcohol induced sighs. I was

relaxed and flirting seriously with the unconscious-
ness of sleep.

Alice, a serious internal medicine resident from
another hospital, who kept long hours and socialized
little, had been less vociferous than the other guests.
I was surprised she even accepted my invitation, and
was not disturbed by her lack of participation in the
group discussions. When she and Ruth, a local laboratory technologist, sat down after everyone else
had left the party, it became obvious she needed to
talk. My lifeless body seemed no deterrent. As my
thoughts lifted in an ether realm, they toyed with
reality as my guest's words pierced my conscious-
ness, stimulating curiosity.

It was easy to arouse my interest. After three
months of living on my own I realized my naiveté.
Achieving a bachelor's degree followed by a medical degree did not ensure worldly knowledge or
maturity. Girls who live at home during their form-
ative years of education are well protected from a
world yearning to impose its experience into their
basic formula. Loving and protective families offer
support and stability that make involvement in other
peoples' lives and lifestyles less important or necessary.

I listened as Alice spoke tenderly of Tara, an
anesthesiologist who worked at one of the other
Miners' Hospitals. In my state of semi-consciousness I remembered her as a young resident with wiry
hair unresponsive to lacquers. Her coffee and cream

complexion suggested generations of white influx diluting her African origins. My eyelids almost popped open as Alice related her intense love for Tara. I controlled myself, however, and continued imitating breaths of somnolence. It became more difficult to sham sleep as I heard of deep passion, infidelity, problems of acceptance, and periods of violent anger between the lovers. Ruth listened patiently, offering no advice as she acted the part of a good sounding board. Alice's serious mood lightened as she unburdened herself to someone else, and, unsuspectingly, also to me. Ruth offered Alice some reassuring words and then suggested they leave, as it was late. Ruth thoughtfully covered me with a blanket as the two left the apartment, locking the door behind them.

I was made uncomfortable by what I had heard, but also curious. I had spent four years as a student in a female medical school and was not unaware of Lesbian relations. Several of our classmates were suspected of homosexual relationships but it was not something we talked about openly. Not until two students in a sorority house were caught in an active sexual act did the rumors gain credibility. We later became aware of Lesbian relationships among a few of our instructors. When the stories surfaced I learned from my classmates, who had lived in college dorms, that homosexual experiences in undergraduate school were widespread. Probably not as common as in the twenties, before birth control was prevalent and women satisfied sexual urges by experimenting with one another. Edna St. Vincent Millay, noted American poet, spent her Vassar years involved in numerous Lesbian affairs while craving and indulging in opposite sex relations as well. Many literary and artistic women during the twenties had sexual exploits rivaling any modern day adventures in homoeroticism.

Yet, in recent times, the unwed female physician seems more suspect than the average single person. I have resented the stereotypical picture of the homely, lonely woman doctor with questionable sexual preferences. I remember speaking to a doctor's wife who was concerned because her daughter expressed a wish to enter the medical field.

"It's not like she is ugly as sin," she said. My response, accompanied by a silent, stony stare, was sarcastic.

"Oh, I didn't realize ugliness was a prerequisite for attaining a medical degree."

Shortly thereafter I sent the daughter an article about a woman voted Miss Pennsylvania in a previous beauty contest who had just been admitted into medical school. I did not hear from her or her mother, but never missed an opportunity to tell the story when her mother's obstetrician husband was present.

As I reflect upon my naïve response to the recognition of Lesbianism between the two women at my party I dredge up memories buried long ago.

I remember having a crush on my female instructor in creative writing as a college freshman. Then, I was frightened by my feelings, wondering if I might have Lesbian tendencies. Retrospectively, I realize this is not such an unusual response, especially for a sheltered young woman with my limited sexual experience, even knowledge, at that time of my life. Actually, my feelings for her may have been the spark that drove my nascent writing career forward. I was so eager to please, I wrote in excess of what was expected simply to gain her favor and attention. Subsequent life experiences proved my heterosexual bent, and the memory of that teenage crush faded, only to be revived when I was uncomfortably privy to that intimate conversation in my apartment.

CHAPTER 6

When death occurred in our hospital the usual procedure was to ask the family for permission to perform an autopsy. If granted, the next step was to notify the pathologist at Harley Hospital to come do the post-mortem examination. Harley, one of the larger hospitals in the chain, employed the only pathologist in the immediate area who traveled to the various hospitals that needed his services.

When I was in medical school and internship the autopsy procedure fascinated me. Knowledge I could learn about the actual cause of death as well as the opportunity to restudy anatomy on a real body instead of the *Gray's Anatomy* tome was a privilege that only the surviving family could bestow. Permission was not sought for my own gratification to have the opportunity to study anatomy. It is the duty of every physician to attempt to get permission for autopsy because hospital accreditation depends, in part, on how many deaths are followed by post-mortem examination. This is especially true in teaching hospitals because pathology conferences are held following each death. The attending physicians and the pathologists discuss how the case was handled and whether anything could have been done to prevent the death. If mistakes were made that were preventable, or suspicious circumstances were involved, hospital accreditation could be withheld.

It was not an easy task to ask this permission of a grieving family, and the rapport the doctor had with the patient and family was usually the deciding factor on whether the autopsy was granted. After I pronounced a patient dead I gently offered my condolences and assured the family that we had done everything possible to help their loved one. I went into details about the treatment we had given and offered several suggestions as to why the person might not have responded. I recommended permission for autopsy be given so we would know for sure what caused the death. Most families kindly submitted when they realized it could not hurt their loved one and it might help another patient with a similar disease.

The pathologist was the sine qua non of the medical profession. With his *retrospect scope* he could usually determine the specifics of why the patient had died and perhaps how it might have been prevented. The clinician spent hours studying tests, examining and re-examining the patient, yet, more often than desired, the diagnosis remained a mystery. At autopsy, the chest and abdomen were literally unzipped and all organs of the body could be seen in their actual state, then examined microscopically. Most of the time an unequivocal diagnosis was made with the ease that an intact body did not allow.

In my pre-clinical years I had spent extra hours in the pathology laboratory watching and assisting at the autopsy table. It was not that I had a special fondness for dead bodies. On the contrary, I am embarrassed to say I was actually frightened to be alone with the dead. In medical school I shunned working in the anatomy laboratory by myself.

As first year medical students we were identified in elevators by the smell of formaldehyde clinging to our clothes. Three or more students in an elevator guaranteed a look of scorn and distaste from upper classmates who held their noses and waited for the next elevator. They, too, had gone through this stage, but we forgot so much time was spent with dead bodies that we became unaware of the odor that hung over us like an invisible blanket.

In anatomy class four students shared one body culled from the unclaimed dead, or donated for study through bequests. These bodies had been embalmed and kept in the morgue for four years before we worked on them. We believed this was to protect the students from disease, and to protect the bodies from our dissection should they be claimed before the four year period. The first day in anatomy class at *Woman's Medical College of Pennsylvania,* fifty-two female physicians-to-be were presented with thirteen bodies to share among them for study. Each body was totally wrapped in white gauze and it was the job of the four students sharing each body to cut away the dressings and wash off the greasy protective film covering the corpse before we commenced study.

I shall never forget watching hair on an arm appear as the gauze fell away from my probing scissors. I shuddered visibly when I realized this was a real body and had once been a living being. No one laughed when three of our classmates fainted that first day in anatomy class. I wondered if this had been a class of men would there have been double the number who fainted? It was a solemn day, working quietly on these bodies wondering who they were and how they ended up on our marble slabs. The professor reminded us of the privilege we were given to study this body, and due respect was warranted. After a few days we respectfully named him "George," but we stopped thinking about his origins and settled down to serious study of his anatomy. He became an object of study rather than a human being, making it an easier matter to deal with. By the end of the year we became so accustomed to dissecting the body we could eat a sandwich with one hand while the other probed the contents of the corpse's abdomen.

However, I never fully conquered my discomfort at being left alone with a dead body. Throughout my years of practice I always insisted that a nurse be present when I pronounced someone dead. The nurse accepted it as protocol; I knew it was cowardice.

On several occasions when Dr. Alan Curry, the pathologist from Harley, came to our hospital to perform post-mortem examinations, I asked permission to assist him. He was delighted to have help, and I was pleased to have the opportunity to study his techniques while I dissected and reviewed anatomy. *Gray's Anatomy* presented marvelous pictures, but unless you could actually feel and trace the blood and nerve supply you never really could study the organ thoroughly.

I learned a lot of pathology from Al Curry, and after many sessions he invited me to perform the next autopsy by myself. I was expected to observe the whole body, surgically open it, remove, weigh, and describe each organ, and chemically preserve each one for his more important work, the microscopic examinations. I was thrilled at the educational opportunity, but I did not look upon critically ill patients as future prospective clients. On the contrary, death is the clinician's most despised enemy. The battle to defeat that enemy is the life-long struggle of all physicians: to conquer, his reason to keep fighting. The battle scars, unfortunately, contribute to egos as large as those of journalists or movie stars.

Webster's Dictionary defines ego as: "the self; the individual as aware of himself. Conceit." There are times in practice when you feel you have total control of a patient. You put your hand on his shoulder and say, "You will be cured, we can work it out and I know we will win." You do not know this for certain, but the statement builds confidence in you and faith for the patient. It is this sense of control that contributes to the sense of ego. I do not believe this is intentional deceit, but rather a method to incorporate the patient's help in searching for a solution to the medical problem. Danger arises if you truly believe you can be dominant over the patient and the situation, as a faith healer might, forgetting the limitations of medical science.

One quiet night, while on medical service, I was awakened at midnight by the night nurse calling to inform me that an older, comatose, terminal patient had succumbed in his sleep. The family, expecting his demise, had already been given the news by the nursing supervisor, and they were en route to the hospital after notifying the funeral director. By the time I arrived everything was ready for me to pronounce death and speak to the family. Permission for autopsy was granted, and while nervous at the prospect of my first solo post-mortem, the anxiety was lessened by the knowledge that this would be a fairly routine case with no unexpected cause of death, and I felt confident I would do a satisfactory job. Then it hit me. I would be spending the next several hours in the morgue, in the middle of the night. The dead Mr. Collins and I would be intimately connected physically, while his spirit hovered overhead observing my snatching his body parts. Of course, I thought this simply to lighten *my* spirits, because I have never considered the possibility of an ethereal presence after death. I believe death ends a life; we live until we die, and that's that. I do not believe in an after-life; I do not believe in heaven or hell. I do believe this great life must be enjoyed to its zenith daily, and we should not burden ourselves with what might follow. I have difficulty coping with death because it makes a finality of life, and I sympathize with those who have passed away because they can no longer enjoy life's pleasures. I also have difficulty with families who find relief that their loved one is "now with his beloved wife," or "now he is free of pain and in heaven." I have respect for their feelings and appreciate the comfort it gives them for their loss but I cannot share their beliefs.

While I digested the scenario of spending the night alone with Mr. Collin's body, I became aware of the appearance of a dapper, smiling gentleman, impeccably dressed in a black suit, a white shirt with black and gray speckled bow tie, and smelling of soap and *Old Spice*. He shook my hand firmly, introducing himself as Jim, from Sturgis' Funeral Parlor. He looked fresh, clean and neat, nothing like the rumpled physician bolted from sleep to spend the night with a cooling, not-yet-stiff body. Unaware the family had given permission for autopsy, he had arrived to collect the remains of Mr. Collins.

"Don't worry," he said between slightly protuberant teeth separated by a wide grin, "I'll wait until you're finished. Be happy to help, if you like. It would be easier than coming back in the morning."

My smile was not as interesting as his, but it reflected relief and pleasure at the prospect of his company. We went to the hospital morgue and wheeled the body to the autopsy laboratory. Jim waited patiently as I prepared the instruments, the scales, and the tape recorder so I might easily speak into it to record my observations and the weights of the organs as they were removed. I felt and acted confident as I made the first incision under the collar bones and into a midline incision over the sternum, continuing down to the abdomen. The crunch of the cutters against the ribs shattered the quietness of the lab but allowed the contents of the chest cavity to be exposed for examination. As the heart was exposed my composure was temporarily destroyed as I involuntarily stopped short when I noticed two weak heartbeats. I knew this was a reflex action of cardiac muscle and it did not suggest the patient was alive, but I was annoyed at myself that Jim might have noticed my anxious response. He was an undertaker, so I was sure he had seen this reaction himself during embalming procedures, but I also knew he probably never flinched when it happened. There is a sense of apprehension when pronouncing a patient dead. I always check that the pupils are dilated and non-responsive to light. I am not satisfied with the absence of a heart beat, and usually thump the chest to be sure the heart will not restart. There have been experiences when death is pronounced and the patient was still alive. I was never involved in such an occurrence, nor do I know of anyone who was, but subconsciously I am aware it could happen. I do not shorten the process of identifying death until I am absolutely sure no sign of life exists.

The autopsy continued with slow and deliberate motions of our four gloved hands working side by side. Jim assisted by holding back skin and tissues so I could dissect and remove each organ, describe, weigh and record my actions. He was a quiet and gentle partner, but I was aware of frequent long sighs I attributed to his fatigue over loss of sleep and my delay in completing the task in a more timely fashion.

When my examination was over, and the body stitched closed, Jim quietly placed the corpse in a body bag and graciously thanked me as he left to deliver the contents for the next step of processing at the funeral home. It was not until the next day, when I spoke to the pathologist, that I learned his task of embalming was made more difficult because I had carefully tied off each blood vessel, as I would have done in a surgical operation. In my attempt to do what I considered a good job, I messed up things for the embalming procedure. No wonder the man kept sighing!

CHAPTER 7

Mattie Ballard was a patient who would teach me a new side of medicine. A local physician from Mayking, Kentucky, had referred her to Miners' Hospital for evaluation of symptoms of weakness, fatigue and a persistent skin rash. It was usual for private doctors not connected to the hospital to refer patients for complete workups because they had no access to laboratories, and the United Mine Workers of America paid for the total care of miners and their families. The choice to use local physicians was still the patient's privilege and many preferred that to the modern and cold professionalism of the hospital facilities. We had good rapport with family physicians and always sent complete reports of any medical procedures done so the patient could continue to be followed locally if he or she preferred.

The internal medicine specialist, Dr. Ted Joad, did a thorough medical history, examination, blood tests and X-rays, and Mattie was scheduled for a return appointment for a pelvic exam and follow-up, which she never kept. The blood tests revealed severe anemia and it was necessary she have further evaluation, but Mattie did not respond to letters and she had no phone. Fortunately, the hospital had invaluable assistance from the Visiting Nurse Society of Kentucky. These women were trained to find patients and explain in lay terms the necessity of following the doctor's advice. The nurses had grown up in the community and knew the people and their families well. Miss Murray, the visiting nurse, went after Mattie Ballard with the determination of a stout mountaineer. Her task was not easy. Mattie lived deep in a hollow of Pine Mountain. There was no road leading to her house, and the closest a car could get was within two miles. The rest of the journey was on foot, mostly up hill. Of necessity the trip had to be made on a dry day because the thick, black mud following a three-day Kentucky rainstorm made these paths impenetrable.

Mattie was an obese black woman with an easy smile and bright white teeth beneath a thickened upper ridge of pale, pink gums. Unlike her female neighbors the presence of chewing tobacco had yet to leave its telltale brown streaks on her teeth. She lived in a two-room shack at the edge of Upper Creek next to a small cornfield terraced up the mountainside. When I went to visit her sometime later I marveled at how the field could be planted and worked in such tight quarters. Characteristic of the area, a washing machine, hand filled with creek water, sat on the front porch and was partially hidden by a clothesline hung with clothing of all colors and sizes. About five hundred feet from the house

stood a wooden outhouse with the door leaning pre-
cariously from a broken hinge. The home was completely surrounded by mountains, the quiet stillness
broken only by the reverberating screams and howls
of her seven children.

As with all mountain women, Mattie's lot was a
hard one. Her husband was a respiratory cripple
after working in the mines for twenty years. An
oxygen tank sat in the corner of one room almost
next to the open fire stove where he sat for hours
attached to the tank by a nasal tube. Finances were
a constant problem, but they managed somehow,
and except for the ubiquitous problem of intestinal
worms the children seemed healthy and happy.

Mattie's life was no different from that of a
white woman living in the mountains. Anti-Black
sentiment existed in Kentucky as it did in the rest of
the South, but was not a major problem. Mattie was
accepted, but had she not been, her smile and cheer-
ful, nervous laugh would probably survive no matter what.

Nurse Murray found Mattie and was accepted
hospitably while she explained the need for her to
return to the hospital. Mattie's reason for not keeping the appointment was simple. Dr. Joad had
explained that she was to have an internal examination, and because he was a man she refused to
expose herself to him. Miss Murray's simple solution was to refer her to the female doctor employed
by the hospital. Mattie was skeptical at first, but had

no argument to offer the persuasiveness of her fellow countrywoman. She set a definite date to be
seen at the hospital.

Mattie's reluctance to be examined by a male
physician was no different than I encountered on
opposite grounds. When I first opened a family
practice in New Jersey the largest percentage of
patients were women, children next, and the most
reluctant, the husbands or fathers. It did not present
too great a problem because I was associated with a
male physician who subsequently became my best
friend and confidant. Dr. Frank and I solved the
problem of patients reluctant to be examined by suggesting he examine my male patients, and I his
females. We were confident that in time, as they
became accustomed to each of us when we rotated
"on call" schedules, they would eventually return as
a family unit. And they did.

Strangely, it was different in eastern Kentucky;
my male patients did not seem to mind being examined by me. I theorized that our scene was so foreign to patients that if they accepted medical care
they assumed it would be on hospital terms, and
they knew no different. Females, on the other hand,
were reluctant because of old mores that men should
not see their private parts.

Thus it was that I saw Mattie Ballard for the first
time in my office. Her history was reviewed and
physical examination completed, including a pelvic
exam. She accepted the latter, but was nervous and

self-conscious. Her children had all been born at home, assisted by a mid-wife, so this internal examination was an unusual situation for her. Further laboratory tests were completed and the final conclusion was that Mattie suffered from iron deficiency anemia secondary to diet.

It was difficult to delve into the medical history of these mountain people. The doctor was an outsider to whom one did not openly reveal personal aspects of life. It took many visits and hours of talking to get the mountaineers to open up and speak freely. They are a proud, honest, and courteous people who answer questions with a "yes" or "no," but avoid personal information not asked of them directly. The local diet consisted predominately of corn, shucky beans, potatoes, and greasy pork back. One of the best dishes I was served at the home of a patient was a delicious hot soup of the dried beans, shucked from dry pods, soaked in fat back and stewed with local collard greens. It was lip smacking good and a dinner I could never produce either because those local ingredients were not easily found in New Jersey, or because the concoction lost stature as it traveled north.

When I questioned Mattie about her diet she admitted to the usual foods, and confessed eggs and meat were neither a daily nor a weekly choice in her menus. I started Mattie on therapy for anemia and saw her at regular intervals. With each visit she became more friendly and talked freely behind her never ending smile. By the end of the third visit I had found the etiology of anemia and the solution to her problem.

Since childhood Mattie had been brought up on a diet that was the strangest her city bred doctor had ever heard. Local physicians were probably more accustomed to regional dietary habits and would not have been as amazed. Mattie told me of a favorite food her mother prepared for the family in Alabama during her younger days. The basic ingredient of the dish consisted of reddish-brown dirt dug from the surrounding fields. It was abundant, cheap, and delicious. The dirt was seasoned with herbs and salt and baked in the form of a pie. It lent itself to a multitude of variations. Most delicious were the balls of dirt prepared with a mixture of corn and tomatoes, then breaded and fried in deep fat. Mattie also liked to eat the soil fresh and uncooked as one would nibble on nuts or crackers. After she left Alabama her craving for this food continued, and family members frequently shipped her packages of the local soil. From this virgin dirt she continued to make the delectable dishes she was so fond of.

The thought of eating dirt did not appeal to me, but I listened quietly in my most professional manner. After all, I was a physician, and I was familiar with the condition called "pica," a craving for unnatural types of food, but I had never previously known a patient who manifested the symptoms. I pressed further by asking if there was anything else unusual in her diet, wondering to myself what she considered unusual. She gave me her characteristic nervous giggle and said she had been meaning to tell me sooner, but did not know if it had any bearing on her condition, an every day occurrence to her but of paramount importance to me. She confessed she consumed about four boxes of Argo Clothes Starch weekly! She ate these firm, velvety chunks straight from the box and had an uncanny craving for them, another piece of evidence for a diagnosis of *pica.*

The cause of the anemia was established, and I climbed one step higher toward a fuller understanding of these strange and fascinating people.

CHAPTER 8

Weekends off duty were like time off from any job: lots of fun. The staff who shared time off would plan ahead to take trips locally or go home for a fast visit. There were times, however, the trip never materialized because the night before turned into a catastrophe. I remember being on call for emergency room duty when two brothers from a nearby town got into a drunken brawl and came close to successfully killing one another. One brother was stabbed in the abdomen and the other had a gunshot wound to the chest. Two operating rooms were actively involved in patching the damage the argument had caused. I was enlisted to assist the surgeon operating on the abdomen of brother number two. At the moment, I did not consider it an honor and was resentful not so much toward the brothers but to the *White Lightning* which had abetted this violent behavior. I could almost smell the sickening, fermented odor of the vile spirit exuding from the abdomen on which I worked.

For the preceding two weeks I had planned this three-day weekend home to Philadelphia. When young and homesick, a twelve hour drive to spend a few waking hours with family before turning around for an equally long drive back did not seem such a hardship. I have mentioned before that during my time spent in Kentucky I was never lonely. But I had never left my city of origin to go away to college, or even medical school. This distance away from my family was a new experience for me and did occasionally result in feeling homesick. I spoke to my mother by phone about once a week, but I missed her closeness, and the smell and taste of her home cooking. We used to compete about which of us made the best apple pie. After observing her technique several times I felt ready to make pies on my own. I told her to go upstairs because I did not need her help. Making the filling was easy; when it came to the crust it was a whole different bag of dough. Her technique of rolling the dough was a progressive work of art that seemed so easy while I watched. The dough flowed from her old, three-foot-long, homemade, wooden rolling pin as if it were controlled by computerized calculations. The draped dough molded itself masterfully over the lumped apples filling the under crust. There were no holes in the perfect circle that unfolded to form a crust whose edges were then sculpted faultlessly into a scalloped pattern. Needless to say, my inexperienced efforts produced an irregular mess punctured by irreparable holes. My wimpy call for help was curtly but only temporarily refused. A mother's love is a rare and forgiving blessing we never fully appreciate.

The most difficult task in getting home was planning three consecutive days off, which I had done successfully. I had not taken into account, however, spending the entire night before my travels swimming around the slippery, glistening contents of an abdomen that was tranquilized by an overdose of homemade booze. I walked off duty that morning sweaty, smelly, tired and limp, as if I had been on an all night alcoholic binge myself. Instead of jumping in the car where my suitcase waited, I staggered to the shower and fell into bed where I had a good, feel sorry for me, cry.

Most weekend trips were less traumatic. For one weekend, several of the doctors and nurses planned a two-day camping journey at Breaks Interstate Park on east Kentucky's border with Virginia. The park rests on both state borders, and the river cuts a deep gorge through the mountain, so it is frequently referred to as the "Grand Canyon of the South." The rim of the canyon affords an exquisite window on the rolling, verdant Cumberland Mountain Plateau. Unlike its western counterpart, this canyon had very few visitors devouring the surrounding beauty and quiet. Our camping area, adjacent to the rim, had a picnic table, wood-burning grill, nearby water supply and primitive, but adequate, toilet facilities. As no one invaded our Shangri-La for the entire weekend, we felt as if we had found a little spot in a stereotypical heaven.

These moments in life when I felt one with nature were memorable and special, and the absence of strangers added a heightened feeling of serenity.

Hideko Yoshino, our Japanese-American gynecology resident, had given us individual lists of foods and utensils to bring for the cookout meals. Everything was accounted for except the butter, bacon, and milk, all of which were resting neatly packed in a plastic bag in my refrigerator back home. Cooking without fat was a small obstacle we overcame with a little ingenuity our forefathers would have been proud of. An omelet cooked with cheese and tomatoes, further moistened with a little Riesling wine made a superb breakfast and was healthier than bacon.

We spent the afternoon hiking through the woods along a small stream with Judi David, a nurse born and raised in eastern Kentucky, as our guide. The early spring air was a panacea for the cooped up tensions of hospital life. Newly budding trees painted a soft green contrast to the brittle, brown, winter-tired branches. The limpid water revealed a multi-colored bed of stones on the creek bottom, and as the water ran rapidly over them soft, musical sounds played like the keys of an instrument. The further along the stream we walked the faster Judi's steps flew until she seemed to be leaping from one large rock to another.

"Hey, Judi, what's the hurry?" shouted Ruth, the medical technologist and the least physically fit of our group of four girls.

"We really have gone deeper into the forest than we should have and I don't want to be here when the sun sets," responded Judi, with a whisper of anxiety in her voice.

I was having trouble keeping up myself, and did not relish the thought of stumbling into the cold creek. Melodious as it now sounded it would be a climactic clash of cymbals should I fall in. As we all picked up our pace to keep up with Judi I noticed that Hideko suddenly took the lead, and even though she was shorter than the rest of us she leaped forward even faster than her predecessor. Oblivious to my surroundings at this point, I concentrated totally on steadying my footing. It was Hideko's voice now calling,

"Let's get going! Speed up, will you?"

"I'm trying," I said as I became more annoyed with the race and the slippery stones. "I still don't see what all the hurry is about."

Shortly we came to a path leading away from the creek and back up the canyon. Halfway to the campsite we came to a resting spot and I finally learned the reason for the speedy exodus. Judi, and then Hideko, noticed snakes were coming out of hibernation and they literally were crawling all over the creek banks. Judi, a bona fide country girl,

knew which snakes were poisonous and which harmless, but decided to leave without a thorough study of their species. She also knew this city girl was terrified of the creatures and decided we should abandon the area as soon as possible. I thanked them for the wise decision. I had been so absorbed in the natural beauty of the woods I, thankfully, never noticed the viperine activity about me or I might have knocked my companions down trying to escape.

Back at the campsite we started preparations for dinner. We built a fire in the grill and while the potatoes baked we cooked a large steak for each of us and accompanied it with a green salad and a glass of Chianti wine. Oh, how delicious it was, even without butter on the potatoes. When we got into our sleeping bags I decided to lie on the concrete path rather than on the floor of the forest to avoid creepy crawlers sneaking into my impromptu bed. We talked quietly under a sky that looked as if it had been pierced by a million silver tipped needles. As sleep pushed me into a lovely state of semi-consciousness the quiet of night was interrupted by a strange scraping sound close to my head. My friends were already asleep and I did not want to disturb them with a foolish fright. The longer I lay there the louder the sound grew. I was sure one of those loathsome snakes was creeping toward me, sharpening its scales along the concrete. Quietly I crawled out of the sleeping bag, rolled it up and walked over to the car. Safely in the back seat of the Nash Rambler I covered myself with the sleeper and snuggled in for a soft, secure night in civilized surroundings.

Throughout my stay in Kentucky other staffers and I continued to voyage to some of the loveliest state parks I have ever visited in my life. Rustic campsites were replaced by heated log cabins with open fireplaces and wood chopped and stacked by the entrance. Well-furnished living rooms opened into kitchens with refrigerators, propane stoves and running water. Real beds and mattresses offered improved sleeping quarters devoid of creeping and crawling bedmates. The gourmet kitchen facilities were unnecessary because the adjoining park lodge supplied lovely meals. The indoor bathroom facilities added a touch of humanity, especially with hot showers. We enjoyed all these amenities at prices well within the range of a medical resident's salary.

The first time I ever went horseback riding was in one of the state parks in Kentucky. It was spring and the first time the horses had been ridden for several months. When my horse was brought to me he seemed as reluctant at the thought of my mounting as I was to mount him. I wore a pretty new tan suede jacket and I felt as if I belonged with the horsy set but I wasn't sure the animal agreed. Two men were needed to help me up, and once astride the horse I felt I was atop a second story house looking down a steep stairwell. The stable master decided to ride close by to help me gain confidence, but because the trail was narrow and uphill he seemed a long way ahead of me. After a short distance the horse halted in the middle of a slimy puddle and repeatedly slapped his foot in the muck, splashing my lovely new jacket with large patches of dark brown clogs of mud. He further embarrassed me by extending a very large fifth leg that almost reached the ground. The groom did all he could to suppress his laughter as he rescued the reins and led me out of my predicament while the extended appendage swung in tandem with the swishing tail.

Some of the trips we took out of eastern Kentucky were about business combined with pleasure. One of the perquisites of being employed by a large organization was that once a year the United Mine Workers of America paid for total expenses for one medical convention and one specialized course anywhere in the country. Raquel Conn, a fellow resident, and I decided on a medical convention in New Orleans, Louisiana, which her father, a general practitioner, also planned to attend. Neither Raquel nor I had ever been to New Orleans, and I must admit we chose the site not for the quality of the convention, but for the excitement of the location. The five-day meeting along with a purloined weekend extended our trip to a full week.

Being employed by a large company had its advantages. If I were in private practice I would have paid all expenses, and probably would not have chosen such a distant site for so long a time. Continuous medical coverage for private practice made travel difficult, but with a salaried position, patient care was uninterrupted. It was also nice to have the assurance of a steady bimonthly paycheck despite the number of hours worked or patients seen. There were no bureaucratic tangles to deal with in hospital administration. Although I was employed by what was essentially a non-medical corporation, a medical doctor ran each individual hospital rather than any union representative. This early in my career, however, I was not interested in the logistics of hospital management. We all had good rapport with the physician-medical director who understood our problems intimately and served our purposes. It wasn't until years later that I found how disruptive hospital management, and especially Health Maintenance Organizations, could be.

When it was time to leave for the convention, Raquel and I decided to drive because of the fall season when the mountainside was resplendent with color. We also wanted to see more of that part of the country, and my fairly new 1957 green and white Dodge vehicle with its sleek, large finned tail made a slick chariot to fly off in. We planned to drive to the western part of Kentucky and then head south through Tennessee, into Mississippi, and finally to Louisiana. The drive through the mountains of eastern Kentucky was slow because the roads were narrow and circuitous. After several hours of tedious driving I was eager to get to main roads and give my car the opportunity to show her speed. I was fantasizing myself seated in a poinsettia-draped courtyard sipping a New Orleans Sazerac, a cocktail made with bourbon, absinthe flavoring, bitters, and sugar stirred with ice and a twist of lemon. I had read about this famous drink and could almost taste it as I speeded to pass a car on a three-lane highway, the first car we were able to overtake for hours. There had been no opportunity to pass cars on the narrow mountain roads, and I wanted to "open her up." It was a foolish decision on my part, because another car was coming toward me in the middle lane and I was going too fast to squeeze back into the traffic line. The imaginary cocktail and my head smashed into the windshield as Raquel's screams sounded over the screech of the brakes while I pulled to the right to avoid the car headed straight at us in the center lane. The impact was on both drivers' sides and in horror I watched the tire on the passenger side of the other car fly off and sail like a wind surfer over a high embankment, thankful it was only the tire and not the entire car and passenger.

The three of us walked away from the mangled cars with no major injuries. I had a left black eye and a bruised left shoulder, Raquel a blackened right eye. We left the wrecked car with intentions to trade it for a new Rambler station wagon on our return, and proceeded to New Orleans by train. Meeting Raquel's father lent stability to our changed circumstance. I had decided not to inform my family about the event, but soon after we arrived at the hotel I received a call from my mother who learned of the accident from the insurance agent searching for my New Orleans address. After all assurances were made we turned our attention to the medical conference, seeing it all through dark colored glasses, an easy compromise to explaining our black eyes.

A couple of days later my fantasy came true. Raquel and I were seated in the exotic poinsettia draped courtyard of my earlier imagination drinking a Sazerac, not at all as good as I had anticipated. As we sipped the drinks, two good-looking gentlemen passed our table and I smiled at them. They were seated two tables away, and after several furtive glances passed between us, the waiter presented us with two drinks sent by the gentlemen. Perhaps they thought we were celebrities hiding behind sunglasses, and asked if they might join us, which upon our approval they did. We enjoyed conversation while drinking until they invited us to join them in touring the nightclubs on Bourbon Street, followed by a visit to their hotel. Neither Raquel nor I wanted the suggested entertainment, and when we removed our dark glasses they seemed somewhat shocked at our eyes turning shades of green, black and yellow. In a rather hasty exodus, they wished us well on our visit to this sophisticated city and left. Shortly afterwards, the waiter informed us they had refused to pay for the drinks and we were stuck with a bill for the two unwanted Sazeracs. Raquel and I chuckled as we realized they probably thought we were two lesbians who had almost knocked each other out in a heated battle. We downed the drinks celebrating our good health and a trip that ended far better than it had started.

CHAPTER 9

It was a beautiful, sunny day following a heavy snowfall, which left a crisp chill in the air. A group of nurses, secretaries and I took advantage of the weather to sled down the slopes at the back of the hospital. We had round, aluminum, lid shaped sleds with handles on each side, the same ones used by children. When seated in the center and holding on to the handles, a slight push from the rear produced a great circular ride down the hill, frequently ending with the occupant upside down and the lid on top of the rider. It reminded me of the side of a hog being placed to cook in a cauldron of frozen liquid. Our shrieks of joyful play brought several of the patients to the windows to join in vicarious fun and laughter.

I was so comfortable warming up in my charming efficiency apartment after our playtime. I enjoyed living alone and was always surrounded with projects. A stack of books sat on the dining table waiting to be read. On an adjoining table a ship model was still in the process of being constructed. My high fidelity phonograph system was finally built and I enjoyed the records and radio that played almost constantly. I liked sipping a drink now and then, but this day neither my diet nor my budget allowed it.

The quiet of the afternoon was soon disrupted by a knock. I opened the door reluctantly and found Judi David waiting to come in. I was expecting her visit within the next few days, but was not anxious to hear the information she brought me. A situation had been evolving and she was the bearer of developments.

Soon after our doctors invaded the territory of eastern Kentucky, the local legislature decided to impose a tax on any new residents who worked in the area, basically a levy paid for the privilege of working in Liggett County. Object: to increase revenues in the local treasury. An absence of new industry in the area meant that the only people being hired were all connected to the hospital. Miners were out of work, and little money came into the area. As recent employees we felt the local government treated the incoming physicians as a potentially lucrative source of income by leveling this form of taxation, and although it was small, we resented it. Most of the doctors opposed the tax, but I could not enlist their support to my side. They knew the tax was small, and as law-biding citizens saw it their duty to pay. I could not abide this decision. I loudly proclaimed to anyone listening that I had no intention of paying such a ridiculous tax, and I was willing to go to jail rather than be subjected to observing this law I resented. It was my nature to take a moral stand on issues. In medical school I was voted the representative to settle disputes between students and staff. During my internship I championed for rights of female physicians. Fighting for repeal of this tax was a challenge I found exciting, but wished I had more support from my colleagues. Being a woman in a man's profession (at the time) made the fight more difficult, but I was getting used to having to fight for survival in a man's world.

Months went by and I remained the only defiant tax evader. The hospital employees' joke was a cup being passed around for donations for my defense. I denounced such help and insisted jail was my way of proving the tax wrong. Surely the local government would not arrest a physician from the Miners' Memorial Hospital. If they did, I would prove my point by remaining in jail while the case brought attention near and far to the illegality of the issue. This was my cause against wrongful authority, and spending a few days in jail could not be such a bad ordeal. It would be a new experience and might even be fun, or so I thought.

With all the noise I made people throughout the town knew of my plans. The workers at the local supermarket wished me luck as they chuckled and shook their heads. Lawyers whom I had met socially strongly advised me to drop the issue and pay the taxes. Local police informed me they would enforce the law and encouraged my support of the tax.

Judi was engaged to Tom Caudill, a big, handsome patrolman, always impeccably dressed in his blue-gray uniform with a crisp, hard-rimmed cap. Tom had pleaded with me to observe the law because it was his duty to enforce it, and he did not want to jeopardize my relationship with his fiancée by hauling me off to prison.

"Rita, we've got to talk," Judi said as she entered my apartment.

"Tom asked me to come tell you what he heard at the police station," she said seriously. "He was the one chosen to either talk some sense into you, or usher you to your new quarters in the brig by Wednesday."

"He can't be serious," I responded.

"Tom is waiting in my apartment to discuss it with you. Let's go see what he suggests."

Tom's idea made good sense. If I were serious about going to jail it was time I visited the jailhouse to check it out. I had never been in a prison before, but from movie descriptions I envisioned a private cell where I could catch up on my reading while my fame spread throughout Kentucky, and maybe even into Philadelphia, as the defiant female physician bravely fighting the establishment without the help of associates. I was ready.

"Ok, Tom, let's go."

Tom chose to drive us in Judi's car rather than his official police car, as this was not yet an official act. We stopped in front of a building different from others only in that the windows had bars, unlike the prisons I had seen in movies, and I lost some of the anxiety building within me. When we entered, however, the raw smell of sweat and other unpleasant odors stopped me momentarily. Tom led the way up a winding metal staircase to a scene I can only describe from memory. When I look back I remember it as a huge pen encompassing the entire second floor of the building. I visualized a monstrous birdcage dropped on the floor. The cage was built of thick iron bars that tapered at the top with an opening like that of a barred birdcage. Perched along the bars were about six or seven disheveled looking men with unruly hair, shaggy beards, and dark overalls. Several were toothless while others displayed loosened, rotting front teeth when they smiled at us as we peered through the bars. These men were the epitome of the term "jailbird." At the center of the cage sat an open, soiled, smelly toilet and near by a tiny washbowl with a communal towel. Scattered around, like perches of grounded birds, were tiny cots with uncovered, dirty mattresses. Odors of vomit, stale alcohol, and urine all congealed in my nostrils and quivered in my stomach. I did not ask if there were separate quarters for female prisoners, and if there were I was in no state to visit them.

We walked quietly out of the prison, deeply inhaling the fresh cold air. As we drove away, I thanked Tom for his help as I whipped my checkbook out of my purse and hastily wrote a check to the tax collector for the overdue $75.

CHAPTER 10

The day was ugly by all standards except mine. Eastern Kentucky had yet to present me a day where I could not find beauty or happiness. When I first decided to come here, the usual trepidations about a new job and new location abounded. The major reason I chose the position was because of indecision and insecurity about my place in the world of medicine. I agonized over leaving the city for a rural practice with a vastly different culture. Would a young, naïve girl from South Philadelphia fit into this alien place? The adjustment I made was quick, easy, and exciting and my choice filled me with pleasure. College was a great experience, but I never had the opportunity to fully enjoy it because I worked hard to maintain my scholarship, and I worked for grades adequate for admission into medical school. This was a nightmare of intense study where I spent little time being part of the world let alone enjoying its beauty and variety. I marveled at the good decision I made to come to this beautiful area, but today I walked from the hospital depressed, my mind full of problems. Bertha Pike was the source.

I entered my apartment and changed into jeans, which finally closed comfortably on the second hook. I yearned to go outdoors to shed my depression by imbibing nature. I walked toward the apple orchard under a solid, monotonous gray sky. The mountains stood black against it, as if draped in a thin layer of coal dust. Beyond the orchard I looked through the trees to the stream flowing below. From this height I felt too close to the hospital so I climbed the rocky hillside to the lonely creek where solitude was guaranteed.

The path was muddy, scissored by deep, irregular furrows from the last rainstorm. Seeking the firmest ground, I walked around the trenches, trampling on small shrubs, which were heroically trying to establish roots. The path to the creek was difficult because dead, broken branches closed it off. I crunched along, trampling those in my way, keeping my eyes closed as I pushed through the taller limbs. The self-made path was softer along the creek where the ground sifted with sand and small pebbles of coal. The bare tree branches threw shadows like thin black ghosts following along the ground while their sister apparitions danced, presenting wavy specters across the water. I stopped by the trunk of a large maple that leaned lazily over the water. The only sound was that of water flowing peacefully over and around the rough stones on the creek bottom.

I drank in the beauty, the odors, the sounds, and

felt my depression lifting. I stared at the water and thought again of Bertha Pike. I was near the end of my two-year employment in Kentucky when she visited my hospital office and I was fond of her from the beginning. Bertha had never been in a doctor's office before that visit. She presented herself on the recommendation of the most informed persons in town – the daily shoppers at the A&P supermarket. These women took the opportunity of their casual meetings over the meat counter to discuss their ailments and how they treated their infirmities. Occasionally they had a good word for one of the doctors at the hospital, even if we were all "furriners." At one of these sessions Bertha heard about the woman doctor with the funny name who was supposed to "know her stuff." She came to see me, and in her simple, open manner told me what she had heard, and felt I could cure her. I was pleased, amused, and humbled, but hid my feelings behind an impassive professional face.

Bertha was a typical mountaineer – pleasant, obliging, cooperative, but not eager to reveal her personal life. She was tall and quite thin with a slight sag to her shoulders. Her hair was completely white and pulled back in a loose, irregular bun while the shorter hairs above her forehead did their own thing. The age stated on the chart was 57, but similar to her kinswomen she looked ten or fifteen years older. Soft wrinkles controlled her face and flowed into warm, frequent smiles. She had lovely blue eyes with a youthful twinkle. Each probing question into her medical history was answered quickly and pleasantly with "Yes, ma'am," or "No, ma'am," and along with the response an affirmative nod or a negative swing of her head. The presenting complaints were vague: recurrent upper abdominal pain. She avoided the word "pain," and with a shrug of her shoulders, screwed up facial expression, and pouting lips, she tossed her ailments off referring to them as "just a rising." This mountain term referred to any medical discomfort from a small boil to a full blown ruptured appendix.

Considerable time and multiple questions revealed a pattern of symptoms, and Bertha finally acknowledged that she really had not felt well for several months.

During her physical examination she remained at ease and pleasant. I could not help liking her, and was pleased by the sense that the feeling was mutual. Some clues in her history made me suspect possible tuberculosis. I ordered the necessary laboratory tests and prescribed a mild antispasmodic. As the diagnosis was not established, the medication was non-specific and I honestly could not expect much change in her symptoms.

I was not surprised when the chest X-ray demonstrated a suspicious lesion in the lung apex suggestive of tuberculosis, activity undetermined. In order to verify a diagnosis of active tuberculosis it was necessary to culture tubercle bacilli from the sputum. The patient, however, was not coughing or actively expectorating so we could not collect a specimen through this relatively easy method. Instead, we would have to hospitalize Bertha, in isolation because of possible active tuberculosis, and thread a tube into her stomach to aspirate gastric washings to culture for the presence of swallowed tubercle bacilli. Hospitalization would not appeal to this patient. I was juggling options when I came across the results of another test; her blood studies were reactive, suggesting that she might have syphilis. My previous probing into her background did not suggest she had the disease, and later, when I questioned her husband, I learned he had never been infected so it was not transmitted through him. Mr. Pike showed discomfort with this diagnosis and was annoyed that I diagnosed his wife with a disease he knew had a disgraceful connotation. I tried to explain the test might be a false positive reaction, which occurred five percent of the time and required additional laboratory tests, including a spinal tap, for confirmation.

I was left with the problem of describing medical problems to a person who had no knowledge of medicine, doctors, or how these diagnoses would impact her life. Bertha had to be told she had tuberculosis, but we didn't know if it were infectious. She had to be told she had syphilis, but we didn't know if this were a definite diagnosis or simply a test result requiring further testing to prove its accuracy. This all sounded confusing to the patient, but thorough investigation was necessary and patient compliance was essential. The biggest complication was yet unknown to me at that time, and probably just as well, for Bertha may never have agreed to hospitalization.

The day for Bertha's return visit arrived and I was determined to convince her to be admitted for further studies. Before she was ushered into the office my receptionist related how pleased the patient was with her treatment and how much the medication had helped. I knew the drug had not produced any miracles. Bertha exhibited a rare and honest faith in her doctor and I was certain compressed sugar tablets, a placebo, would have yielded the same effect. Bertha agreed to hospitalization. How humbled and pleased I felt, and how I hoped the right decisions would be made, for I longed to have her faith in me continue.

I was still so young and new in this field that my insecurities overwhelmed my abilities, and patient approval was the spark that gave me confidence. I do not believe there is ever a feeling of being totally competent in medicine because it is not a specific science. There are always worries of inadequacy or whether the problem was handled in the best manner with the least physical invasion. Relief of pain and suffering is what the Hippocratic Oath guarantees, not cure. It is the art of medicine, not the scientific meddling, that helps the patient, and this cannot be taught. It must come from experience and an inner, deep desire to help. Some people might call this divine intervention; I think of it as a self-driving force. Medical school does little to promote self-confidence because it takes the scientific approach with which humanity cannot compete. For me, my defining moment came when I was 50 years old, and was asked by the medical administrator at my hospital to enter a teaching program for family practice residents. At first I was afraid I was too far from book knowledge to compete with the feisty, know-it-all young students. The administrator assured me it was my experience the young doctors needed, not facts. Each month that I worked with the family practice residents my confidence in my own abilities grew. Teaching them what had become second nature to me: joint injections, physical diagnosis, familiarity of skin lesions, and patient communication skills, gave me a heightened feeling of competence and confidence I thought I had never reached before.

Oh, what misery I put poor Bertha through in the hospital. She was isolated in one room, and invaded by a steady stream of nurses, aides, and laboratory technicians, all clad in gowns and masks because of the possibility of tubercular contagion. She was given the works: daily gastric tubes, spinal tap, blood tests, and X-rays. Yet, every morning when I made rounds, she greeted me with a pleasant smile and sparkling eyes.

"Doctor, you sure done me a lot of good since I've been in the hospital. I ain't never felt so good."

What great thing was I doing for this lovely woman? I was just giving her vitamins and trying to establish a definite diagnosis by wringing her through an array of unpleasant procedures. Her husband made frequent visits to my office inquiring into her progress. Mr. Pike was a pleasant chap; a miner disabled by a back injury. He, too, had blue eyes, but they lacked Bertha's twinkle. His smile was wide, interrupted by crooked, dark brown, stained teeth. He was grateful for all that was being done for his wife, and told me,

"You know, she calls you her little doctor and says you sure are helping her. She thinks a whole lot of you, she sure does."

It was not long before all the reports were back with the discovery of Bertha's most serious problem. The routine Pap smear of her cervix was finally read by the pathologist and reported as suspicious of carcinoma of the cervix. Now I had to tag another serious diagnosis on a poor uneducated mountain woman who had come to the doctor with only the equivalent of a bellyache.

Again I had to approach Bertha with the problem of inconclusive evidence. We had to do a biopsy of the cervix to be sure of a diagnosis of malignancy. It amazed me that Bertha did not lose her patience or her temper at this point. I had made three major diagnoses, and could not prove any one with certainty as yet. She could have asked what good were all these tests when they proved nothing, would this nonsense ever stop, and would we ever be sure? But, she only smiled and said,

"Doctor, I'll do anything you say, but I'll never be operated on."

I tried to explain that the operation was minor and quite simple. If she did have cancer it was early and could be cured, but the operation had to be done. Her final answer was she would never agree to surgery now or anytime in her life. I approached Mr. Pike for help in convincing Bertha, but he said he knew her since early childhood and when her mind was set, "there ain't no a' changin it."

All these problems surrounding Bertha had caused the depression that sent me down to the creek to sort out. I suddenly realized my feet were damp and cold and the mountains looked a few shades darker. I do not know how long I had been standing on the bank looking at the water, but a soft rumble of thunder in the distance helped convince me it was time to leave.

It is now 40 years since I was involved in the life of Bertha Pike. I look back on it as if it were yesterday and can still feel the warmth of her smile. I had to leave Kentucky before her entire case came to a conclusion, but certain facts I do know. Bertha indeed had active tuberculosis and, as was the custom in the fifties, she had to be hospitalized for treatment in a local sanatorium. She did not have syphilis. The blood test had been a false positive and she had never been infected. Her husband was especially pleased with this diagnosis, for I do not think Bertha ever understood the significance of the disease. The follow up for treatment of the possible carcinoma of the cervix was lost to me. When I left she was still refusing further investigation because surgery would never be an option. She and her husband at no time shed further light on why she was so frightened of surgery. Perhaps someone in the family had a poor experience and Bertha identified with the result. I called the hospital several times after I returned to Philadelphia but she had never reappeared for treatment and the medical records office was unaware of the outcome of her case. I like to think there was more to Bertha than a diagnosis of tuberculosis, syphilis, and cancer, and even though I never saw her again I felt fortunate to have been able to include her in the deep humus of my life experiences.

It is always difficult to leave patients in mid-treatment, but it happens often. Whether working in the ER, or covering another physician's practice, patients come in and out of one's life, frequently making follow-up impossible. The patient may not return to the physician, or perhaps was on route to a distant location. I wondered how the disease process played out, but I never knew. A patient once signed himself out of the hospital after I admitted him from the ER with a diagnosis of an acute heart attack. Against all urging, and despite thorough explanations about his condition, he refused to submit to treatment. I was horrified and guilty because I could not convince him to do the right thing. Legally it was his decision, and there was nothing further I could do. I never learned what happened to him, but the lesson I did learn was that I had to stop thinking about it and move on.

Involvement in patient's lives becomes more difficult when I had a close relationship. Family practice is not like psychiatry where personal relationships are taboo. As a family practitioner in a limited practice in a small community in South Jersey, many of my patients became (and still are) my closest friends. I learned where to draw the line to keep my feelings from interfering with medical decisions. Complications arise if the relationship becomes more physical. I had three affairs with married men originating from our medical association. I preferred married men because I was not looking for a permanent relationship or to break up a marriage. They were fleeting, clandestine, and exciting events, and no one was hurt. When I sought judgment from a married female friend about these affairs her encouraging words were, "It's better to do it with a friend rather than a stranger."

In Kentucky my relationship with patients was more formal because of social mores and my youth. I accepted the respect these mountain people afforded me as "doctor" meekly and with pleasure. I afforded them the same respect when I visited their homes on a social basis, but the distance between doctor and patient was too vast to allow for genuine friendship. My memories of these good people, however, will last a lifetime.

CHAPTER 11

An unusually quiet day in the emergency room gave me the chance to listen to nurse Polly Perkins tell me stories about her miner husband Ross. He was one of the fortunate ones who still had a job and brought home a weekly paycheck, which, coupled with Polly's earnings, made their economic standing in the community higher than that of the average coal miner family. They had been married only one year and had no children. Polly came from a family of eight and was not eager to bestow the frustrations of her childhood on to a second generation. She wanted more out of life, and the job with the Miners' Memorial Hospital, along with an employed husband, promised to offer her advantages she did not have growing up. Her new car was a joy and gave her the freedom to shop in the big town of Pineville, Kentucky, where she could buy almost anything she wanted. Years of living with the uncertainties of a coal miner's existence however, kept her grounded to save some money for the future. Her father had not been so lucky and lost his life in a mine disaster when she was young. Fear of losing Ross in a similar disaster was a constant cause of anxiety.

Polly's comments gave me moment to reflect on one of the most prevalent non-infectious diseases of miners' wives, anxiety-depression syndrome. When I first started practicing in the area, life seemed lost in time simplified by the lack of distractions of the outside world. There were no television sets, practically no radios, few cars, and no movies. Life revolved around the family and home. The only pleasure couples seemed to share was creating children, which they did in profusion. I thought the freedom from world news, lack of education, and closeness of family would produce an anxiety free and happy existence. Absent from my equation, however, was the constant state of worry to which the woman of the family was subjected. She worried whether her husband would return from the mines and, if he were unemployed, would welfare funds be sufficient for their basic needs. Paramount in all her thinking was when would black lung disease incapacitate her husband.

I treated many women with long lists of non-specific complaints that fit no diagnostic pattern. I remember being amused and winking at the nurse in disbelief at my first experience of quizzing a woman who complained about backache. At whichever part of her body I pointed she described pain; each system of her body I inquired into functioned poorly. Finally I pointed to her big toe and asked if this too hurt. Her large, sad eyes staring disapproval made me realize what a stupid ass I was. My high and mighty attitude had bypassed the patient's need for understanding and help in what proved to be a severe case of depression. This experience made me realize how arrogant a newly minted physician can be. My mind was an oasis of brilliant medical knowledge, overflowing with facts and diagnoses, but my haughtiness came close to causing me to miss the patient's depression. I was embarrassed by the recognition of my problem and was glad it taught me a lesson so early in my career. After my first week I learned to shut my mouth and listen. Many years later I passed on to student general practice residents that a good diagnosis could usually be made without a multitude of tests if the physician took the time to listen to the patient and to digest thoroughly the history, then follow with an equally thorough physical examination. It is a lesson all physicians should learn and practice early in their medical careers. The result was my reputation as a surrogate psychiatrist grew over my years of practice. Patients realized that I was willing to give them time to listen to their problems, and soon I was being invited out to lunch on a regular basis. The price of a meal was far less than that of an office visit or the fee for a psychiatrist, and the patient could talk in a relaxed environment. The kudos: the more history I learned from a patient the better able I was to make a proper diagnosis, and I earned an even more rewarding reputation (at least to me), that of a good diagnostician.

I got distracted because of Polly's anxiety over Ross being in constant danger as a miner. I laughed when she continued her tale to tell me that the first monies they spent were to build an outside shower for Ross. When he came home from the mine he looked like a cloud of coal dust had burst over him, covering every inch of his body and clothes with a fine layer of black powder through which only two white eyes were visible. He was refused entry into the house until he shed his clothes and showered while Polly placed his clothes in the washing machine. They were fortunate enough to have electricity and running water so the job was easier than for most.

I had never been inside a coal mine and asked Polly if Ross would give me a tour. I did not know until then that miners considered the presence of a woman in a mine to be extremely unlucky. Somewhere the tradition started that if a woman entered a mine it was certain a mine disaster would follow. No one seemed to know where this belief originated but they all honored it. Polly herself had never been inside the mine, and while she never actively sought entrance, my interest in going stimulated hers. She invited me to dinner on the following Sunday, knowing the mine would be closed, and hoped she could talk Ross into taking the two of us there.

When I arrived at the Perkins home I was immediately struck by the difference from the homes of older, unemployed miners I had visited. House calls were not part of our hospital duties but I visited patients socially whenever I was asked. Their homes were so different from those I was now familiar with. I had been raised in a relatively deprived area in south Philadelphia, although I never realized it. My grandmother's three story home bordered the Italian Market and housed several families. An outhouse in the back yard had been replaced by an indoor facility when I was very young. Clothes were hand washed in a large tub in a shed adjacent to the kitchen. Tin ceilings, Victorian stained glass chandeliers, a wooden ice-box, and a coal fired kitchen cook-stove were exciting, nostalgic memories; they did not represent poverty to me. The miners' one or two room sparsely furnished shacks spelled deprivation and abject poverty, but somehow I felt comfortable while I subconsciously compared their homes to those stored in my childhood memories.

The Perkins home, on the other hand, was a modern one-story building on a flat piece of farmland where Ross raised corn on his days away from working in the mine. I was graciously received, and knew Polly was very proud that this home was so different from the one in which she had spent her childhood. Not too many miners were this affluent or educated, and this young couple was proud of their accomplishments. I had already grown accus-

tomed to one-room wooden shacks up in the
"hollers" as the typical miner's home so this was a
pleasant surprise, especially since my visit did not
have to be limited to three hours for fear of having
to use outhouse facilities.

Dinner started with the typical home brewed
beer. Ross did not make his own, but it was easy to
purchase it from any backwoods mountaineer, and
the drink was always a marvelous harbinger of a
home cooked meal. Polly prepared a delicious ham
from a freshly butchered hog raised by a neighbor.
Fresh corn and roasted potatoes replaced the greasy
collard greens and shucky beans I had grown so
fond of, but were equally as good, especially accompanied by home made biscuits and red gravy.

Now that the meal was over I was eager to visit
a coalmine. Ross was prepared to honor our
request, but he was a miner, and still superstitious
about women in mines. Without further discussion
he courteously ushered us into the car and drove to
a dirt road that was closed off by a chain barrier. We
left the car and walked a distance down a lonely,
dusty road to the entrance of an old abandoned
mine. Ross smiled and said we had not mentioned
whether the mine had to be functioning, and he
thought this old mine would be more exciting to
visit. He opened a rusty lock with a key extracted
from his back pocket, and as the creaking wooden
door opened inward a blast of cold, stale air mixed
with the smell of motor oil assaulted our faces. Dust

rose tickling the hair of our nostrils. The wide path became increasingly narrow and steep as darkness slowly swallowed the outside light that had seeped in. A beam from Ross' flashlight penetrated the darkness and came to rest on an old iron wagon used to carry coal along rail tracks in the mine. I was thrilled to extract from it a few pieces of shiny black coal the size of bookends, which is how I eventually used them.

The light flashed on wall hooks on which several miners' hard hats rested, alongside old yellow coats covered with black dust. Two more rail wagons lay abandoned against a dirt wall supported by beams. Several feet ahead I saw a cage elevator in which two or three men might fit, and on the right was a long black tunnel, its end not visible in the projected light. The dust loosened a loud sneeze from me, which echoed through the shaft and was followed by a wheezing creak off in the distance. In the dim light my frightened eyes met Polly's as our hands clasped in anticipation of impending disaster.

"It's time to go," said Ross quietly. "Those old beams are dry rotted, and remember, you are women!"

Later I realized he was probably building tension to give us a thrill, but at the moment I was happy to pocket my "mined" coal and high tail it out of there. My coal bookends are still a prized possession, safely preserved in a thin layer of shellac. As far as Polly and I know the old mineshaft never suffered from the presence of our estrogen, and may still be there.

I knew very little about eastern Kentucky and the mining industry before I went there. I was a typical medical student unaware of life outside my solipsistic existence. Too much time was spent in the medical field. I was deprived of knowledge of the rest of the world, but did not lessen my ignorance because there was no time. It took me years to learn that time is not something you have but rather something you make. Once I applied that perception my life changed. I realized I could do absolutely anything I wanted in life if I really had the desire. This revelation led me to fascinating pursuits throughout my life. My dreams of traveling the world turned to reality. I became a multi-media artist, a photographer, a poet, and a writer. I made myself achieve just to prove to myself I could. I did not excel in all these endeavors, but the thrill was in the journey, and in the high it produced.

Ross explained a lot about the miners and the area, which I had not previously known. His evaluation of the situation and his revelations came as a surprise. Ross, and others in eastern Kentucky, offered information that helped me better understand the political and economic problems of Appalachia. He spoke knowledgeably about the plight of the coal miner in the Cumberlands, and how the companies had ravaged the area of the best coal veins in the mountains. The companies then turned to strip-mining, which destroyed the timber and mountainsides, leaving streams polluted and timberlands devastated, he explained. Large coal companies kept all the wealth for themselves and none of the profits were poured back into the communities to build new schools, hospitals or facilities to improve the social structure of the local towns. Ross believed that as the coal was ripped out of the countryside so, too, were the souls of the workers living in company camps, as they saw their paychecks becoming leaner with each passing year. Those who wanted better opportunities for their children left the area in search of finer schools. The youngest and brightest abandoned eastern Kentucky while the oldest, poorest, and sickliest remained behind, losing dignity and ambition as they surrendered their total existence on welfare.

Ross explained that the only part of the coal industry to help the miners was the United Mine Workers' of America, which had built the marvelous chain of hospitals providing excellent and free health care while also offering retirement benefits to their members. I never became involved in the political struggles of the people during my employment in eastern Kentucky. It was not until 1963, when Harry M. Caudill published his book, *Night Comes to the Cumberlands*, a Biography of a Depressed Area, that I learned of the history of Appalachia. My life in Kentucky was spent growing as a person and as a physician, and it was not ıl years later that I became involved and interested in its history.

An important man in the history of the struggle of coal miners against the bureaucracy was Joe Begley, of Blackey, Kentucky. Joe had fought all his life for miners' rights and against land destruction by strip-mining. His sympathies were with the workingman and he fought against big industry, coal operators, and discrimination. When I visited Blackey, during my year as a resident, it was a ghost town with few people, few homes, remnants of an old coal mine and an abandoned railroad. The most exciting place was the C. B. Caudill General Store. A tall, lean, bearded fellow who closely resembled Abe Lincoln ran it. The gaunt man was Joe Begley, and his store was packed from floor to ceiling with all sorts of antiques, hardware, and foodstuff, the latter a small part of the inventory and the only items that were really for sale. The store was a tribute to and a museum of the history of eastern Kentucky. I took many photos and spent some time talking to Joe learning more about the region. I met Joe Begley once again in a1995 book, *Coming of Age,* by Studs Terkel, where an entire chapter was devoted to Joe's thoughts and views on the coal industry, community, and life in general. I was proud to have had the opportunity to meet him many years earlier.

CHAPTER 12

Almost everyone knows Dickens's *A Christmas Carol*, and can probably easily picture Tiny Tim hobbling about on his crutch. When I first saw Tom Jenkins I immediately remembered Tiny Tim because they were about the same age and both used one crutch, but the similarity ended there.

Tom arrived in the emergency room accompanied by his mother, Effie Jenkins; the image of the two will forever be imbedded in my mind's eye, especially because of what followed. Blood was flowing profusely from Tom's nose while his mother held a thin, bloodstained towel under his nostrils. The child looked pale and weak; his mother was tired and worried. Tom's left knee was bent and fixed at a sixty-degree angle and supporting him under his left armpit was a hand carved wooden crutch with no arm padding. I knew it was hand crafted because the wood was rough and irregular and not finished with sealer or paint. The wooden bar on the crutch that supported his hand was slightly tilted off center and looked shiny from long use. As he walked around the emergency room the tip of the stick pounded quietly on the linoleum tiles, the noise softened by cloth and twine padding wrapped around the bottom of the crutch to keep it from skidding on smooth surfaces.

My nurse assistant was helping in another room so I proceeded to set up a tray to pack Tom's nose to stop the bleeding after the simple techniques of pressure and ice failed.

"How did this happen, Tom?" I asked, expecting he had fallen or gotten into a fight.

"Oh, it just come on," he replied.

"No fights with a friend?"

"No, it just comes."

"Do you get nose bleeds often?"

"Oh, yeh."

Mrs. Jenkins sat quietly next to Tom holding his hand. I wiped away blood inside the nostril looking for a broken blood vessel on the septum of the nose, the most common cause for recurrent nosebleeds, but the bleeding was too steady. I set about packing the anterior part of the nose with gauze and while waiting for the pressure to stop the bleeding I continued to talk to Tom.

"How long have you been using the crutch?" I asked.

"Long time," he said.

"What happened to your leg?"

"Oh, been that way a long time," he offered.

I was used to short, disinterested answers from the mountaineers, but I thought it might be easier talking to a child. It obviously was not. I turned to

Mrs. Jenkins and asked,

"What's the problem with Tom's leg?"

"It ain't no problem," she responded, "it's just part of everything."

My eyebrows furrowed, but just as I prepared to get more deeply involved in my questioning the gauze became soaked with blood and my attention turned to replacing the pack.

"I think we ought to do some blood tests on Tom," I suggested to Mrs. Jenkins.

"Ain't no need to," she responded.

"This is not normal bleeding," I said, "we have to investigate further to determine the cause of the bleeding."

Tom and his mother both stared at me as if I were some alien from another planet. I knew the mountaineers were ignorant of common medical maladies, and generally showed little emotion even if they felt deeply. I wondered why they were generally so reticent. Were they disinclined to speak only in the presence of medical personnel or was this a more widespread characteristic? I reasoned that the life of a miner's wife was difficult. She was poor, unfamiliar with the world outside her immediate environs, and under constant stress. There was probably not much to speak about that would interest anyone so she chose instead to remain silent. Her emotions were restrained because of pain and rejection, and repressing them was a form of denial. The fear and sadness in the eyes of these people as well as their body language spoke what their tongues could not.

I was concerned that Tom and his mother might not fully understand the significance of the problem. Just as I started to offer an explanation the nurse returned, quickly evaluated the situation, and called me aside.

"I'm sorry, I didn't get his records to you in time; Tom has hemophilia."

Another blow to my ego! Again, as I continued to do throughout my practice of medicine, I thanked my lucky stars for nurses and their invaluable assistance to doctors. Nurse Polly knew Tom well from his frequent visits to the emergency room, and had I seen the chart the diagnosis would have been obvious. Whether I would have diagnosed his condition on my own is questionable; hemophilia is a rare disease. It is a bleeding disorder characterized by a deficiency of certain proteins in the blood clotting system, and is inherited as a sex-linked recessive abnormality. Hemophilia occurs almost always in boys and is passed from mother to son through one of the mother's genes. Most women who have the defective gene are carriers and exhibit no signs or symptoms of the disease.

Defective coagulation is present at birth and serious or fatal hemorrhage may occur in the neonatal period, often following circumcision. Internal bleeding is the most serious complication of hemophilia, but bleeding into joints is painful and damaging. The pain can be so severe that the patient may be reluctant to use the limb, and repeated bleeding causes irritation to the joint leading to arthritis and deformities. Blood fills the joint space, and because of coagulation problems aspiration of the joint is frequently contraindicated. If the blood remains in the enclosed joint space it eventually causes damage to the tissues and bone. Scarring, along with immobilization, results in permanent deformity. Treatment of the disease, at the time, was limited to transfusion of fresh plasma to correct the coagulation defect temporarily.

There must be some form of angel designated to oversee young doctors, not only to protect their patients from harm, but also to keep inexperienced physicians from destroying themselves with self-doubt. My angel succeeded in stopping the blood with only a little help from me. Effie nodded her head in thanks, but when she turned to Polly I discerned a faint smile, which I accepted as an equal "thank you" rather than one of amusement over my nearly missed diagnosis. Tom bounced off on his crutch looking very much like Tiny Tim, happy to leave the hospital without further treatment.

As I watched Tom scurrying away, I asked Polly if the hospital would supply him with a new, modern crutch to replace the precarious one he used. She smiled and said they had tried several times, but Tom never used the new one given to him. His father had made the old crutch; Tom was comfortable with it, and apparently saw no need to change.

CHAPTER 13

One evening Abbey, a technician from out of town who lived in one of the apartments, had a party and everyone was invited. We had a grand time eating, drinking and laughing. The invited locals always managed to have plenty of home-brew on hand, and we city folk drank it with the same gusto as the distillers, although it rattled our brains faster than those who were exposed to it all their lives. One of the guests, Dot Collier, a nurse's aid at the Miners' Hospital, was her usual humorous self. She congregated with a small group in a corner of the apartment whispering and then laughing loudly. When I looked toward them their eyes turned away and I felt I was the brunt of their laughter, but I did not know why. Little did I know what was in store for me.

I cheated in medical school twice. The first time I cheated was in the Physiology laboratory. We were doing experiments in which an animal was to be anesthetized and operated on, for what reason I no longer remember. Half of the class was to use rabbits and the other half rats. I had the misfortune to draw a rat to be my very first surgical patient. This may not seem much of a problem for a blossoming scientist to attack, but I had and still harbor a most abnormal fear of rodents. I am not sure where it originated, but I do recall as a child running around the kitchen screaming after I saw a mouse.

"For heavens sake," my father called after me as I ran from the room, "you have nothing to worry about. You already stepped on the mouse and killed him," which only made me scream louder and longer.

I am unable to look at mice or rats in magazines or on television and have to avert my eyes until someone tells me they are off screen. Midway into my practice years I learned my secretary had a similar fear. The Eastern Pennsylvania Psychiatric Institute, adjacent to the medical school, offered a program to cure abnormal fear of rodents by slowly subjecting the patient to closer and longer exposure to rats over a two-week period. We both considered going for the treatment, but the longer we thought of being so close to rats the more repulsed we became, and finally we opted out.

So when I came head on with my rat phobia in medical school I knew there was no way I was going to work on this creature. Even with his white coat, he was still a rat. I surreptitiously finagled the papers given me for the experiment until they found their way to a rabbit recipient. I wandered off happily with the rabbit while an unsuspecting student became the proud owner of my repulsive rat. I never confessed my action, and again felt no guilt, assuring myself the other student was far better equipped emotionally to handle the problem.

At the apartment complex on the hospital grounds in Kentucky the residents shared a communal trash area at the end of the building. Some of my friends from Philadelphia knew of my fear of rats and warned me not to approach the trash area after dark because someone had seen a rat there. Dot Collier laughed when she saw me walk far out of my way not to pass the trash cans. She and her four brothers lived in a holler not far from the hospital. An exciting venture for them was to trap rats and take them to the woods where they released and then shot them for the sport of it. She did not understand that I could really be afraid of rats, and offered to take me on their next shooting trip. I politely declined, while hiding my disgust at such an idea. Every time we met in the hospital she'd smile and say,

"You really should come with me and the boys. It's such fun to see how many you can shoot in the shortest time." She had lived in the country all her life and honestly thought I was joking when I told her I was afraid to look at a rat. Dot was fun to be with, but I did not enjoy discussing a subject I hated and tended to avoid her company. Seeing her at the party was the first time in a while that we had been together.

After leaving the party I walked to my apartment, changed my clothes and got ready for bed. I could still hear the muffled sounds of the few remaining party members in the nearby apartment. After a short time there was a knock on my door. I knew it had to be one of Abbey's guests so I opened the door in anticipation and almost dropped over in a dead faint. There at the entrance stood a smiling Dot holding a large cage of screeching rats right up in front of my face. My heart stopped momentarily as I ran screaming hysterically to the back of my apartment. Uncontrolled cries choked my breath as I locked myself in the bathroom. The screams brought neighbors running into my apartment. Even the security guard from the hospital arrived to investigate the horrible scene. A terrified, apologetic Dot left with her cage, still in disbelief, but rightly appalled at the trauma she had caused.

Following the rat episode I thought perhaps God was getting back at me for the cheating episode in medical school. Then I began to worry what He might have in store for me for having cheated a second time in school. The second cheat was when we were required to do a gastric analysis test on ourselves. Each student had to swallow a long rubber tube connected to a metal end the size of a large olive. The metal end went into the mouth and as it was swallowed the rubber tube followed, ending in the stomach where it was to reside for at least an hour. The gastric juices were then extracted from the rubber end that sat in an embarrassing manner at the corner of a drooling mouth. Tests were performed from these juices for the evaluation of ulcer patients to determine the amount of hydrochloric acid in the stomach.

It was a terrible procedure. Each time I swallowed the olive, more closely resembling a huge submarine than a martini olive, it got stuck in my throat and I retched and choked until the olive and its umbilical tube were regurgitated. Over and over the submarine tried to dive only to resurface among sounds like the barking of harbor seals. I spent an entire hour over the laboratory sink trying to get the bastard to float down my esophagus into my stomach. My face colored a deep red, my eyes watered from retching, my throat was scratched, my voice hoarse, and my stomach ached and growled, but success evaded me. The laboratory instructor walked by, shaking her head, while she offered suggestions on how to get the tube down.

"Keep trying," she smiled. I looked at her with bile exuding from my mouth as well as hatred from my eyes.

"To hell with this," I whispered to myself as I threw the tube in the sink and sat in the far end of the room where no one could see what I was doing. I hovered over the laboratory desk feigning work on gastric contents never raised from my reluctant stomach. No sympathy came from instructors or fellow students, so I proceeded to fake my results of the analysis, promising never to order this ridiculous test on a patient for the rest of my life. And I never did. Fortunately, more humane tests were developed in subsequent years, but I never forgot the horrible experience, nor did I feel much guilt from cheating on this experiment.

CHAPTER 14

Obstetrics was my least favorite subject in medical school. I blamed my dislike of it on the stern, white haired professor who was always perfectly dressed and coiffed, and kept her head raised at a level where her nose seemed to be sniffing us in disgust. She was a well-known, highly qualified Philadelphia specialist in Obstetrics and Gynecology, but not as popular among her students as she was favored by her patients. She drilled us relentlessly. My feeling was that midwives had performed these duties since my female ancestors living in caves were delivered of their babies, and they never had to learn all this nonsense. One of our classmates, Nebbowa (Nebbie) Nwozo, had been a midwife in Nigeria for years before coming to Woman's Medical College to study medicine, and while she agreed with me, we also knew this "nonsense" was indeed essential.

In the Obstetrical Laboratory we practiced delivering babies on a life-sized plastic model of a female torso molded from the neck to the knees. "Mabel," as we fondly called her, had no arms, and her thighs were fixed in the delivery position while her abdomen had an opening through which a baby could be placed. Her perineum, the area between the genitalia and the anus, was a large rubber patch with an opening through which our hand entered to determine the position of the baby's head and through which the baby was delivered. The baby was an actual infant cadaver that was kept in a formaldehyde solution between classes. It was essential to use a real specimen because we were learning to feel the fontanels, the infant skull markings, in order to determine the position of the baby for a proper delivery. Over and over we practiced delivering the baby. More accurately, we practiced calling the proper position of the fontanels because the professor quizzed us repeatedly as she repositioned the baby through the abdominal opening on the model, trying her best to trap us by placing the head in a questionable position, as indeed God himself might have done in a real delivery.

I did finally conquer the proper positions, but when we advanced to human specimens I was never comfortable in determining the degree of dilation of the cervix by rectal examination. The nurses in the labor room were far more qualified to know when the patient was ready for delivery. They assisted the students in examining the patients and listened when the students decided it was time to go to the delivery room, but after having delivered so many patients in the labor room the nurses or the attending resident made the final decision about when the patient was to be delivered. Needless to say, I was one of the students who delivered a patient in the labor room bed, and lived in constant fear of doing it again.

Despite my negative feelings about this specialty of medicine, one of life's most exciting experiences is to watch another life being brought into the world, especially when you are just observing the procedure. It is absolutely magical to stand behind the obstetrician and watch a head covered with hair pushing open the birth canal. The perineum thins out to a lovely pink crown as the head pushes outward revealing a moist, pale, grayish face with closed eyes and a shriveled up face. Over the noisy shouts of the doctor and nurses urging the patient to push down, and the mother's muffled screams in the background, this funny little creature proceeds to pound its way through a reluctant canal. Once its ugly, molded head comes out it rotates easily until one shoulder and then the other slides out. Suddenly, in a quick slimy exodus, the entire body swoops out to the rhythmical twist of the doctor's hands as he holds the baby upside down by its tiny blue feet. A slight slap on the behind and the ugly creature becomes a screaming, pink, beautiful miracle. In all honesty, the thrill of being the doctor who delivers the baby is excelled only by the delight of the mother who actually produced this miraculous event.

When I applied to work in third world countries, the only positions offered to me were in the field of obstetrics, and I knew I would reject them.

However, my Kentucky experience didn't relieve me of those important practice obligations. Obstetrics was always somewhere in the background to cause me discomfort and trauma in my practice of medicine.

I hate being awakened in the middle of the night by the shrill ring of a telephone. The irritating sound rattles my brain so my thought processes become confused. I sometimes feel I could lose my way, physically and mentally. In my new apartment, when I reached out to stop the noise, the phone was not beside my bed – that was in my other home. In this new place the phone was away from the bed so I actually had to get up to answer. I learned to do this early on because it would have been so easy to slip back into the comfortable arms of sleep if the telephone were answered in a recumbent position. Is this the night Joseph was to call?

I finally stilled the telephone and shook my thoughts back to the present. Of course, it was not Joseph on the other end of the line, but rather a disturbed obstetrics resident, Hideko Yoshino, calling on me to help deliver twins from a patient who had just arrived in the emergency room with no previous prenatal care. The attending obstetrician had been called out of town and Hideko needed an additional pair of hands. Mine happened to be free at the moment. Hideko and I had been fellow students at Woman's Medical College in Pennsylvania, and while she knew how I felt about obstetrics she insisted this would be a fun experience, as we did not often deliver twins. In any event, I was the only one available and she urged me to get there fast. As long as she was calling the shots I felt it would indeed be fun.

I quickly jumped into my green scrub suit and white hospital shoes, and ran the short distance from the apartment. The black sky looked as if Billie Joe had riddled it with buckshot allowing luminous sparkles to peer through the holes and almost light my way.

I reached the delivery room and scrubbed at the modern sink just outside the doors. The nurse greeted me instantly with a sterile gown and gloves. The brightness of the delivery room with all its new equipment, instruments, and brilliant lights was in stark contrast to the old operating rooms at Episcopal Hospital in Philadelphia. John L. Lewis had spared no money in furnishing this medical facility to be equal, and in many instances, superior to the big city teaching hospitals. The miners might be poorly housed and hidden in the mountains, but the hospitals built to service them were state of the art. The efficiency and training of the nurses also equaled any I had previously known.

Hideko, a very short woman, looked even smaller between the pregnant woman's thick thighs. Hideko shouted to me that the babies were tiny and coming fast. Suddenly, Hideko twisted her body to get into position, and as the baby pushed, more

131

accurately leaped, out of the birth canal she caught
it just like a running back on a football field. I posi-
tioned myself as a wide receiver just in time to catch
the second soft, oblong ball that fell into my hands.
The gasps from the nurses, mingled with a soft cry
from the mother, acted like the cheering section for
the pleased and successful players in this strange
game of delivering life.

My obstetrical skills were called upon far more
frequently than I wished because emergency room
duty meant being available for any hospital crisis.
Midwives performed most deliveries at home in
eastern Kentucky. The complicated ones, however,
ended up at the hospital. This meant our staff had
not followed these patients for prenatal care and had
to be prepared for any medical circumstance. The
obstetrical department was available for the care of
these patients, but the emergency room physician
could be called to assist at any time. Emergency
Caesarian sections frequently necessitated help, and
I always enjoyed the surgical excitement of these
operations. The speed with which the surgeons performed the section was amazing. Cutting into the
uterus was like releasing a zipper from which blood
spouted everywhere. From this red sea a blood covered infant was quickly rescued and deposited into
the open hands of the attending pediatrician. The
speed and dexterity of the surgeon approximating
and sewing the uterus together kept bleeding to a
minimum. I could not help remembering my seam-

stress mother quickly sewing up the back of my father's split overalls while he wore them so as not to interfere with his laying fresh cement. Granted it was an unlikely simile, but one cannot always control thoughts that rise from a hidden psyche.

I experienced another obstetrical fiasco while on ER duty in the middle of a cold, snowy, mountain night. A tall, thin woman with a soiled green kerchief around her head came into the emergency room looking pale and weak. Her husband, who appeared to have dressed quickly by throwing on his coal-dust covered clothes, supported her on one side while another woman stood behind them holding a bundle of clothes. My sense of smell is very acute and serves me well in culinary instances to distinguish various food ingredients and herbs, but offensive odors are equally pungent and overwhelming. A scent of old blood and feces hung above the group. Despite the constant flow of patients coming through the emergency room, the area was always clean and sterile in appearance. The ubiquitous coal deposits on miners rubbed off on chairs and walls, but the nurses and cleaning staff worked diligently to keep the facility spotless. When I came to Kentucky I expected the housekeeping personnel to look like the stereotypical hillbilly one met in the movie, "Deliverance." I conjectured this from the type of people who usually staffed the least skilled positions in city hospitals. It was very different in eastern Kentucky. The few unskilled jobs available at the Miners' Hospitals went to the best qualified of the large unemployed population, not to the few unfortunates who traded jobs for living quarters as they did in Philadelphia hospitals.

"How long have you been bleeding?" I asked the patient.

"I reckon a while," she continued, as I helped her on to the examining table. The nurse and I quickly removed her clothes as we checked vital signs and prepared for a pelvic examination. It was obvious she had just delivered, and a piece of the placenta exuded from the vagina. As soon as I inserted a speculum a huge clot fell out followed by a gush of blood. On abdominal examination the uterus was expanded and soft. I had to cause it to contract to stop the bleeding. The nurse handed me a pair of arms length obstetrical gloves while she ran to get an injection of the oxytocin I ordered to stimulate contraction of uterine musculature. With my right hand high up into the soft, boggy uterus and my left hand massaging the top of the uterus through the abdominal wall I was able to manually cause the uterus to contract and stop the hemorrhaging.

The bleeding was under control so now I could get more history from the patient. This was her seventh child, but she had never hemorrhaged before.

"This 'un came very fast," she said, "I thought I only had to poop, but thar she whar."

"Where's the baby now?" I asked.

"Right thar," she pointed to the bundle of clothes

in the other woman's hands.

The nurse and I stared in disbelief. We had been so concerned in caring for the mother that neither of us suspected nor were we told that the bundle of rags was indeed a living newborn! As the story unfolded, the mother had felt an urge to defecate following a contraction pain and went to the outhouse. As she relieved herself she realized that the baby dropped out of her and into the waste below. She grabbed the cord and instantly scooped the baby out of the toilet opening. Her husband and the neighbor quickly washed the child in a tub of water, wrapped her in some blankets and brought her along to the hospital.

Both mother and child were admitted to the hospital and did remarkably well. The same could not be said for the attending doctor and nurse.

When I walked out of the hospital I was glad it was still snowing lightly. The crunching sound of my shoes on the soft white carpet added a rhythm to my short walk home, and the crisp air cleansed my nasal passages of the previous offensive smells. The changing seasons in this part of the world made me think of Joseph and how he hated the winters. He was used to the tropics and never experienced snow until he came to Philadelphia. He liked warm weather and looked comfortable even as his very black skin glistened with moisture. His brilliant white teeth were a charming presence when his wide grin revealed them, and allowed a dark pink tongue to run across his large, beautiful lips. He was a tall, lean, attractive man whose beauty was enhanced when he wore native costume made from Ashanti Kente cloth from Ghana. He always eschewed his western business suit for African clothes when we went out together because he knew it pleased and excited me.

I missed Joseph so much since I came to Kentucky. Outside of medicine he was such an important part of my life when I was an intern. Nebbie, my Nigerian roommate during internship, was married to Joseph's brother, Saka. The brothers were also from West Africa, but from the neighboring country of Ghana. They were the children of an extended tribal family unit where to marry outside the tribe was tantamount to heresy. To marry someone from another country, albeit just a few hundred miles away and still in West Africa, was grounds to be disowned.

Joseph and Saka underwent tribal rites as children and still wore the scars on their cheeks identifying them as belonging to their father's tribe. During their childhood, however, they converted to Christianity when a missionary group offered an opportunity for a free education. Later, the government of Ghana sought the best students and accorded them an education in America if they, in turn, donated up to ten years of community service to their country upon return. It was an opportunity hard to ignore and the brothers ended up in the

United States, Joseph pursuing a business degree, and Saka one in arts and music. Nebbie was offered the same opportunities in neighboring Nigeria, and came to America to study medicine.

The African students met in Philadelphia where Nebbie and Saka eventually married, and Joseph met and married Aleia, a fellow student from Ghana. The mid-fifties were exciting times for these students. Ghana was gaining independence from England and African spirits were high with national pride. I was swept into this general camaraderie, and although Joseph was already married I fell very much in love with him.

When I got into my warm apartment I immediately stripped off my clothes in the small dressing room of the efficiency apartment and jumped into the shower. After drying, I wrapped myself in Joseph's old Dashiki I had purloined from his apartment. I curled up in my small bed stroking the rough, colorful Kente cloth until I dozed off.

CHAPTER 15

Sexual harassment, sexual discrimination and the liberated female are terms that are used too frequently today, I believe, and perhaps also in the past. I remember, as a young intern, complaining to my superiors that I was already liberated and therefore entitled to live in the same residential area as the male interns and residents.

When my internship started in 1957 at Episcopal Hospital in Philadelphia, a new wing was being added to the hospital to house interns and residents. In the meantime, the female staff was housed in an ancient building on the hospital grounds. We were four women on staff and, as we rotated night call, frequently only one female was living alone in this behemoth for an entire weekend. It wasn't too bad most of the time, but when an occasional mouse terrified me by parading around the living room looking for crumbs (or entire sandwiches) left by the mentally challenged strange janitor with roving eyes, the house became weird and lonely.

I shared a room with Nebbie, my medical school Nigerian classmate who also decided to intern at Episcopal Hospital, and felt safer when she was there. The problem, however, was adjusting my sensitive nose to the odor of the chemicals she used to straighten her enormous crown of wiry hair. No amount of grease or chemicals were able to change the stubborn Afro-kink from heading like steel drill bits in any and all directions. The odor subdued me, but never the hair. Although the house was large we were forced to share bedrooms because the other rooms were used for storage and other uses. When I complained to Nebbie that the compound she used on her hair was totally offensive to me, she simply laughed and said, "I'm just doing my best to look white." We both laughed at the foolishness of the comment because she was the blackest woman I had ever met, and a patriotic Nigerian, loyal to her race and country. We joked frequently about Black and White relationships and racial intolerances. I remembered how upset I was when we went to a conference in Maryland and she hesitated before entering a restaurant.

"Do you think they will let me in?" she said very seriously.

"Don't be ridiculous," I exclaimed. "Why wouldn't they?" I honestly had forgotten she was black and that we were in the South. Fortunately, we were seated without incident, because I am not sure what I would have done had we been refused entrance. Joe always joked that the only difference between him and me was that he was born at night and I in the daytime and God colored us in that fashion.

Halfway through our internship the quarters were finally completed and we moved to the new hospital wing. The women were given four small bedrooms at one end of the hall, separated from the rest of the floor by two large, locked doors. The male interns and residents occupied the other side of those doors. Numerous bedrooms were available for the much larger male staff, but the kitchen, lounge, television, radio and small personal laundry room were also on their side. The women were not given keys and were strictly forbidden to "cross over." It was, understandably, the fifties, but four strong, medically trained, multinational women (an African, an Indian, a Filipino, and a white American) were not going to sit this out quietly. We presented ourselves en masse   at the office of the medical director shouting liberation and female rights. The lock was eventually removed from the door, but we were requested to knock before entering. We never did, and if we caught any of the men with their pants down so be it because we had as much right to the facilities as they.

I confess that this call for liberation was also used in a reverse sense. If I did not wish to do a particularly unpleasant task it was not unusual for me to cry, "I'm not liberated, don't give me that job; let one of the men do it." It did not threaten me to be treated like a frail woman at those times, and because of the decade we were in we got away with this double standard.

141

When I was a young practicing physician in southern New Jersey the term "sexual harassment" was not used for the circumstances that today are labeled as such. As the only female physician in the local hospital, both the nurses and I were subjected to repeated unwanted sexual advances by some of the male medical staff. One of the senior internists frequently pinched me and caressed and hugged the nurses. These advances usually took place in an elevator. The older nurses and I slapped his hand and laughingly called him a "dirty old man." The younger nurses were more resentful, but only smirked while rolling their eyes and shaking their heads. I considered these male acts a form of flirting, but never harassment. In return, when a male physician was working on charts at the nurses' station, I frequently clasped him around the neck and left a lipstick-marked kiss on his bald head. We both enjoyed these interchanges and neither felt sexually exploited. I am well aware of the serious differences between harassment and flirting and its connotations, but over the years perhaps the pendulum has swung too far. In any event, this document is not the place for a serious discussion of the matter.

My first experience of being amorously approached by a patient occurred in my medical office in eastern Kentucky. Tim Higgins was being treated for hypertension and chronic obstructive pulmonary disease, and this was his third visit. Tim was a retired coal miner, short and rotund with a round, smiling face supported by a double chin. Bushy eyebrows topped wire-rimmed glasses, and accentuated wrinkles pressed tightly at the corners of his eyes, created by constant grinning. He was quick to remove his shirt and sit at the edge of the examining table. The exchange of air in his lungs was poor due to his pulmonary disease, but this did not stop him from giggling, almost inappropriately, when the stethoscope brushed across his exposed nipple.

"Heh, heh," he laughed and winked at the same time, "That tickles."

His head turned toward me as I moved around to listen to the posterior portion of his lungs. I distracted him by having him repeat numbers and cough while I listened intently with the stethoscope. He was enjoying this examination too much, so I encouraged him to replace his shirt quickly and move to the desk to discuss his medications.

In an instant I had a flashback to a patient I was examining while a student in Urology Clinic in medical school who did not experience Tim's pleasure. At that time, the instructor was teaching me how to do a prostatic massage. He told the patient to bend over and was showing me how to place my gloved finger into the rectum and press firmly on the prostate gland from one side to another. That patient also turned his head in my direction only to bolt up instantly, shouting as he pulled up his pants and ran out of the clinic, "No goddamn woman is going to stick her finger up my ass." My male instructor was sympathetic and apologetic when he saw the horrified look on my face. He warned me men were still not used to female doctors, and I might run across this type of behavior frequently, especially as a young doctor.

"Remember, it may be difficult for some men to adjust to intimate examinations, and you have to learn to accept it," he said kindly.

Women instructors in medical school, however, were not as polite when confronted with a similar occurrence. If a male patient rejected a student's examination while a woman instructor was present, it was not unusual for her to tell the patient to shut up and let us get on with our job. The patient, seeing her a mature and authoritative presence, did as he was told. I sympathized with the males especially when we were required to perform thorough physical examinations, including an accurate measure of the length of the penis using a ruler. No wonder a spontaneous erection resulted. I would quietly cover the eruptive area with the bed sheet, leaving the impression of a tent pole supporting the sheet. Prudently I advanced the examination to another distant anatomical spot, such as the foot.

Tim listened with a quiet smile while I inquired about his diligence in taking his medications.

"'Course I take 'em regular, but they's no real difference how I feel. I thought they woulda made me breathe more easy."

I tried to explain the best we could hope was the damaged lung would not worsen or affect his heart. As I ushered him to the door I inquired about his wife.

"Oh, she's right fine, I reckon. I told her about you, and she said she'd be right pleased to meet you. How 'bout you come to lunch with us? My wife is a good cook. What er she puts on a hog or beans it makes 'im awful good."

I was very eager to learn more about the miners and to visit the homes I saw up the hollers, so I accepted without hesitation. Tim smiled broadly, and before I knew it he had me in a bear hug. Had I not turned my head strategically he would have placed his full mouth on mine. I firmly struggled out of his hold, laughingly proclaiming I could not be his guest if he persisted in this kind of behavior.

His whole body relaxed as he looked at me sheepishly, and apologetically shook my hand. He assured me that he and his wife would be delighted by my visit, and we proceeded to set a date. I felt confident there would be no recurrence of any physical contact as we both placed the matter behind us.

There were several episodes during my years of practice when I had to dodge advances from male patients, but I always treated the matter as a flirtatious, unimportant act, and remained firm in preventing recurrences. Patients generally continued to be polite and respectful. As I got older, however, I found it more difficult to keep *my* distance from male patients. The male body is far more beautiful to me in comparison with the female's. The firmness of masculine skin supported by thick, rippling muscles and either kinky or smooth hirsuitism made tactile examination a pleasure I tried to hide behind a cold, indifferent façade. When I examined male genitalia I was glad my eyes were diverted because I honestly believe there is nothing more pleasurable than to palpate that area of the human body. The soft, loose skin nesting cool, smooth, egg-like testes is an anatomical miracle surpassed only by the awesomely incredible penis with its inimitable erectile tissue. My descriptions may cause some to label me with penis envy, but I prefer to be judged as medically, albeit sensually, objective. At a urology seminar I once attended I remember commenting to the presenter that urologists always seemed to be happy, pleasant people. "Why shouldn't we be," he responded, "all we do is handle genitalia, and we even get paid for it."

On one of my days off I visited Tim and Grace Higgins, but planned to spend no more than three or four hours at their home because I did not want to use their outhouse. It was a beautiful day so I started early in the morning and took a long detour over Pine Mountain. The top of the mountain offered a marvelous vista over hills covered with gray-green evergreens spread like an undulating verdant blanket. The green trees ended in deep pockets of cotton clouds settling in the hollows along with the

morning dew. The town, hospital, houses and mead-
ows were totally hidden under the settling fog,
which completely obliterated sound, coal dust and
poverty. This was as close to heaven as a human
could reach during life.

I spent the morning driving and hiking over self
made paths through the mountain forest. After
relieving myself in a privately dug station I proceeded to the Higgins home. I pulled off the road at
Higgins Holler, parked the car beside a stream, and
walked up a well-worn path as Tim had directed.
About a half-mile up, the trees gave way to a neatly
terraced garden of corn, potatoes, and tomatoes.
Tobacco drying in the barn hung like golden drap-
ery. Up high on the hillside was row after row of
string beans. There was never enough level land in
these hollows so the farmers planted up and over the
hills, reminiscent of the vineyards in the south of
France. The crops apparently did well, but I wondered how much work went into the terracing and
cultivating of these vertical fields. At the foot of the
adjacent hill sat the Higgins homestead. It looked
like most of the other homes within the eastern
Kentucky foothills of the Appalachian chain. The
house was built of unpainted wooden slabs placed
vertically and topped with a tin roof. A wooden
porch ran the length of the front of the house, and
curtainless windows flanked either side of the
entrance. A wooden washtub with a hand wringer
sat on the porch next to two rocking chairs. About

Doctor

M.D.

...eet from the house stood the privy, a
...ved in its wooden door.

As I approached the house Tim came out and
proudly introduced me to Grace who smiled a broad
welcome. She was small in stature with teeth too
big for her tiny mouth and face, which was crowned
with lovely soft, wavy white hair. She wore a loose
fitting blue star-studded dress topped by a red half
apron tied around her waist.

I find it difficult to visualize the interior of the
house, although my recollection of the people and
places in Kentucky is very vivid. I believe my
memory of the house has been tainted by recently
having watched Rory Kennedy's award-winning
1996 documentary film, *American Hollow*, which
depicts a home in eastern Kentucky's poorest
region, and chronicles a year in the lives of a family
living in Mudlick Hollow. I realize now that the
parents of the clan shown were the generation I
treated when I practiced there, and the forty-year-
old offspring were those I either delivered or treated
as infants. Unfortunately, neither has progressed
much from their welfare state of the1960s.

As clear as my memory allows, I entered the
Higgins home directly into the living room where a
pot-bellied stove sat in the center of the room.
Several chairs, a small davenport, and a wooden
table cluttered with folded clothes, completed the
room's furnishings. Behind the living room were
two small bedrooms, one of which had housed the

Higgins' three children, now grown and off on their own. To the left of the living room was a comfortable kitchen with a small pitcher pump for water, a wood-fired metal stove for cooking and a long wooden table with benches on either side. A kitchen cabinet held dishes and glassware.

As soon as we sat around the kitchen table, Tim served warm home brewed beer in small mason jars. The jars added a nice touch to the beer I had grown so fond of. To this day I occasionally still serve beer in small mason jars. They are more difficult to find because my basement is no longer lined by all the jars my mother used to preserve tomatoes.

We talked for some time about living in Kentucky, and how much better their lives had become since the Miners' Memorial Hospital was built. They were honestly appreciative that our doctors had chosen to come to their part of the world to work. They asked a few questions about the doctors in general, but I steered the conversation closer to their lives because that was my interest, and it seemed safer to be less personal about hospital matters.

Grace drank little beer and busied herself preparing the table. What delicious food was to follow! From a huge black iron kettle she scooped out large portions of pork cooked together with shucky beans and collard greens. On top of the fragrant mixture was a thin layer of hog grease that added lip-smacking pleasure. No one I ever knew was able to produce this dish outside of Kentucky until years later when I ate with a black patient in southern New Jersey. Grace gave me a second portion, along with my requested fat back to chew on, before eating freshly roasted ears of corn. Homemade corn bread from an iron skillet accompanied this succulent feast.

Following the meal my hosts showed me around the farm and presented me with some of the gathered vegetables. My visit had lasted three and a half hours, and it was time to depart or use the outhouse. I chose to leave, and found my short, unwanted romantic encounter with Tim had blossomed into a long-term friendly relationship with the Higgins family.

CHAPTER 16

The brain is the human body's most amazing organ. The mind can travel over a lifetime effortlessly, from medical school to eastern Kentucky, with only a flip of a page or a touch of a pen.

On a lovely day in early fall, Ruth, the medical technologist at Miners' Hospital, and I, set out for the countryside because we heard it was sugar cane harvest time. Some of the locals had told us a neighborhood farmer ran a sorghum mill where we could watch the progression of sugar cane to sorghum syrup. Ruth, a country girl from Arkansas, loved the sweet syrup and had my taste buds stimulated for a savory adventure.

Ruth gave me a short introduction to this foreign substance. Sweet sorghum is syrup made from the juice of sorghum sugar cane. Colloquially it is called "sorghum molasses," but molasses is actually a by-product of sugar crystallization from the juice of sugar cane, while sweet sorghum is a variety of a sorghum sugar cane plant. Sorghum is lighter in color and taste than molasses, but heavier than maple syrup, which is thin and has a distinctive taste. Because of reduced production, most of the sorghum was used for forage, but a good proportion was also used for syrup. Sorghum cane, Ruth told me, looks like corn without ears, and instead of a tassel on top like corn, it has clusters of seeds. After the cane matures, it's a labor-intensive procedure to harvest it. The stalk is cut off close to the ground so all that remains is a 5 to 10 foot stalk one and one-half to two inches in diameter and one-half to one inch diameter at the top. At this point the cane is ready for the mill.

In eastern Kentucky there was always at least one regional farmer with a cane mill and facilities for cooking the syrup, and neighbors who shared the resources. We found the farm recommended to us, and spent the rest of the afternoon participating in the festivities brought on by the yearly production of this lovely, sweet syrup.

This community event included several of the neighboring farmers who brought their stalks to be processed. Ruth and I were welcomed as if we too had transported crops for participation in this proce-dure. About a dozen men and women walked around the farm. The men were dressed in baggy overalls, the women in colorful gingham dresses covered with dark blue or black aprons. Smiles revealed teeth loosened from swollen, red gums. There were deep guffaws roaring from heads thrown back in laughter. We were cordially accepted as we introduced ourselves as hospital personnel. Some hands were extended in greeting, while others eagerly passed us mason jars brimming with home brew. The mountaineers were delighted to show us around the farm and explain the procedure of making sweet sorghum.

The rollers in the mill crushed the stalks, and squeezed the juice out of the canes. The juice was then strained to remove pieces of stalk and then collected in containers to be cooked. The liquid was poured from the containers into a huge iron kettle over a wood fire and cooked until it boiled actively for some time. They warned that this part of the procedure was most important. Remove it too soon and it was not done. Wait too long and the end product was too thick and strong tasting. Experience and frequent tasting was the secret for success they told us. While cooking, the syrup was skimmed. One woman stood on one side and another on the opposite side of the large black pot holding skimmers running across the top of the cooking juice to remove impurities. I chuckled to myself as I envisioned witches brewing a bubbling potion in a cauldron as we stood around it, talking and drinking beer.

Each person held a long piece of sugar cane, obviously the upper part of the stalk because it was only about one inch in diameter. Repeatedly we each dipped the stalk into the boiling kettle of sorghum, brought it up to our lips, and after blowing on it to cool the syrup, we licked it clean. After a few minutes, the stalk, wet from our saliva and breath, was returned for a fresh dipping sample. The physician in me tried to reason that the dozen or so people dipping into the syrup with contaminated sticks was not a good idea, especially in a place where tuberculosis was an endemic disease. Nevertheless, Ruth and I dipped along with the others in a frenzied pace of dip and lick, enjoying every minute. This unsanitary procedure was much like a crudités dip at a party where celery and carrot sticks get bitten into with the sauce, then go from the mouth back into the dip. The sorghum tasting at least occurred at high temperatures eliminating all but tuberculosis bacteria. Ruth's eyes sparkled with anticipation as she commented, "Wouldn't this be great over hot biscuits!" One of the other women stated, "All my kids says they don't like it on cereal, but 'course now, they loves it on bread or in cookies." The brew was eventually declared done by one of the elders, and tasting came to an end.

The scene transported me back to my grandfather's cantina in south Philadelphia. I was not too young to join in the camaraderie of his dozen or so friends filling the basement around his nine barrels of wine, although I was too young to participate in the serious tasting of the Beaujolais Nouveau that flowed from the barrel spout into sampling glasses. Two or three glasses were passed among the cognoscenti. Each paesano sipped, and either nodded approval, or screwed his upper lip up into his naso-labial fold in visual disapproval of declaring an end point to the fermenting wine. Grandpop's long mustache probably added some flavor to the wine, but his Italian friends did not seem to mind as the glasses circulated among them. The final decision about whether the wine was just right took longer than that for the sorghum. Several rounds of tasting were necessary, adding to the intensity of jubilation. The women sitting in the parlor upstairs were soon invited to share their opinions with the "official" wine tasters. Of course, when Italian men invite women to their festivities it means food is the entrance ticket. And so it was. Big flasks, covered by woven straw, were filled with the new wine, as the party overflowed to the upper floor. Large pots of water were put to boil for pasta, and a quick, simple, home preserved tomato sauce was emptied from jars. Before long spaghetti with the marinara sauce was served to all present, soaking up the excess wine.

No food followed the sorghum festivities, nor was it necessary. Everyone had a good time, and we were sent away with a bottle of the fresh syrup to use as we wished. Ruth could not wait for the next day to pour it over her morning oatmeal, as she was accustomed to do in Arkansas. I was eager to make sorghum cookies to distribute among my neighboring apartments.

It amused me to think how often I compared my experiences in eastern Kentucky to my childhood in south Philadelphia. The Italian-American experience is as foreign to the Anglo-Saxon mountaineers as wine is to "white lightening," but similarities struck me frequently. A psychoanalyst once related a story about an intensive group therapy session, which he provided for his patients. The five total strangers in this group spent an entire weekend together revealing their most intimate thoughts, reliving positive as well as difficult life experiences together. They bonded as they had never done with anyone before. Years went by with no further contact, until one day the doctor recognized one of the patients across a room. When their eyes met they ran to each other, hugged and cried in a long and emotional embrace. They had once shared something so intimate no one else could understand, and the sentiments they felt were deeply imbedded and unforgotten. While not a perfect comparison, I feel this same attachment to unknown Italian peasants from whom I originated. I am drawn to visit hillside towns in Italy where I can relate to the heritage and roots of my parents and grandparents. I feel this same connection to the mountaineers of Appalachia. While our peasant bloods never mixed in the old world, I feel a closeness similar to what the psychoanalyst explained. Perhaps the roots of all peasants extend deep, searching nourishment, finding mutual compassion and camaraderie, in their varied heritage.

CHAPTER 17

Our hospital in eastern Kentucky was a close-knit community. I often wondered if the other doctors who came there to practice did so for my reasons. I was not ready to decide what to do with the rest of my medical career and felt unready for private practice. Group practice was not as popular as it is today so it was not an option, and most family practitioners started individual practices and remained solo for the rest of their careers.

My over-protected life at home extended through my years as a medical student. The class of 1957 at Woman's Medical College of Pennsylvania started with 50 women students closely supervised and intensively trained. We were competing in a world of male physicians who did not accept us as equals. Our totally female medical school, the first and only one in the country, was dedicated to producing the best the profession could beget. With the small number of students in the class individual attention was far easier than it would have been in a larger, male-dominated medical school. The instructors demanded perfection and worked closely with each student to achieve success. The dropout rate at the end of four years was only five students while larger schools had a much higher percentage of failure, especially in the first year. Their matriculation rate was high because they expected to thin the numbers by failing students after the first year. The Woman's Medical College enrolled the students they hoped would graduate successfully, and this goal was generally achieved.

If a student were headed for failure it was guaranteed to happen in Pathology class. The professor used the Socratic method of teaching, by which we were bombarded with questions and badgered into making logical conclusions. It did not work on students fresh out of college, in preclinical years, who were terrified by the professor's bullying methods. Repeatedly she warned we were being spoon fed the learning, and if we intended to cross Jordan, her analogy for the hospital part of the medical school, we must work harder. One student failed the curriculum at this early stage, and another sought psychiatric help. The professor's more considerate assistant, who had ten children of her own, provided needed support and help, or perhaps more students might have failed.

The supervision I refer to was the effort of the personnel of the college to prevent us from failing to achieve our goals. Just as my mother wanted me to succeed, so too did the faculty, even if, as with the Pathology professor, their methods differed. Special sessions were granted to help weaker students, and guidance counselors were available to deal with personal problems.

In a school with only fifty students, we were well known to the instructors. Frequent social interactions between faculty and students was the norm. Receptions at their homes occurred regularly, with friendly discussions on a more intimate level. At one time, an internist invited three of us to tea at her home. I was impressed when welcomed into her lavish apartment by a uniformed maid, where a fireplace sparkled as if ignited by the classical music playing. The room was lined with books, and the antique furnishings added grace and charm to the tea ceremony. On other occasions staff members invited students, giving incoming women the opportunity to mix socially with upper-class students, in congenial and memorable gatherings.

On some occasions, social activities with other medical schools in the area were promoted so we could meet male colleagues. In our senior year we had a dance and cocktail party with the graduating students of Jefferson Medical College in Philadelphia. The first martini I ever had was at that party, followed by another, and perhaps a third. After spending the rest of the night draped over a toilet bowl watching olives spiraling down into a porcelain tornado, I swore off martinis for the next twenty years.

In retrospect, I feel the extra attention we received as students may have made us more vulnerable, once released in the outside world. One of the reasons I went to the Miners' Memorial Hospital was to have the opportunity to continue supervision in a group-like practice while I decided which direction to finally adopt. I was insecure about my capabilities, and the three other classmates who joined me in Kentucky felt equally apprehensive about undertaking the responsibilities of a primary care physician in a private practice. We knew we were well trained, and while we chose an adventurous path we were aware of our inexperience. Male physicians on the other hand, in my opinion then and now, have enormous egos and testosterone surges that contribute to audacious risk-taking. I believe the production of estrogen helps to make a female physician more compassionate, gentle, and nurturing. In general, a woman physician is as good as any male physician, and often better. This is indeed a sexist remark, but sometimes it must be voiced if only to negate, or equalize, the more prevalent opposite view.

This discussion brings to mind *The Woman's Medical School Creed*, which, I believe, is appropriate to interject here:

Daughter of science,
pioneer
Thy tenderness hath
banished fear,
Woman and leader
in thee blend,

Physician, surgeon,
student, friend.

I feel privileged to have been a graduate of
Woman's Medical College. I feel even more privileged to have started my practice in the Miners'
Hospital in Appalachia. My close relationship with
patients, and the time given to their care, taught me
skills that lasted a lifetime. The art of listening and
touching was the most important of these skills, and
one that is unfortunately no longer part of the average physician's practice today.

My experience in Kentucky lasted only two
years, a more finite time period. The relationship I
had with patients in New Jersey differed because I
practiced in an area that was my permanent home.
Patients who are also neighbors produce more intimate friendships lasting many years, going beyond
a professional bond.

I have kept in touch with many of these patients
since I retired from private family practice in New
Jersey, and the recurring complaints about their current medical care are distressing. Doctors' offices
have lost their personalities. The office staff is too
busy to talk; they do not inquire about other members of the family because they do not know them.
The assistant who sees a patient today will most
likely have been replaced by the time of the next
visit. Doctors zero in on the patient's complaint
with little interest in anything non-medical. Many

young doctors seem reluctant to have the patient undress. Extensive and probing physical examinations are replaced by a barrage of laboratory tests and X-rays costing more than the down payment on a new house. A teenager told me it was no fun to visit the doctor anymore. "We are just a number; like waiting in line at the deli counter."

My consultation room resembled the office in Norman Rockwell's painting "The Doctor." In the thirty-seven years that I practiced medicine in a small suburb of southern New Jersey more time was spent listening to patients than instructing them.

Both my treatment rooms had two comfortable chairs and small desks in addition to medical paraphernalia. The patient was relaxed and able to discuss problems freely. When perched upon an examining table heart rates increase and fear conquers reason. Listening to a patient in a comfortable atmosphere provides insight that results from a thorough examination. People supply enough information through discussion so that, given time, the diagnosis becomes evident. Not only can talking clarify symptoms, but discussing other factors in patients' lives alerts the physician to psychological or psychosomatic issues.

Current medical offices are devoid of chairs in treatment rooms because the presence of furniture hampers the rushed entrances and exits of staff, while a stark atmosphere discourages verbal communication. To satisfy the current vogue, defining dress in medical offices has been abandoned for the sake of political correctness. However, to the patient, a nurse's cap made her responsibilities clear. Now, uniforms no longer define hierarchy. The ubiquitous scrub suit obscures the profession and professionalism of attendants. While having their privacy invaded, patients wonder if the person attending them is a doctor, nurse, aide, or janitor. A major problem in hospitals today is the absence of the crisp, starched, white uniform and cap signifying not only authority but also school of origin of yester-years nurses. Because of the identical dress code, a patient may ask the maid who cleans the toilets the same questions she asks the head nurse because there's no way to distinguish between them.

When I was an intern in the fifties a wise old family physician taught me that touching was the most important part of patient care. Chiropractors achieve success and frequent return visits because of their consistent physical contact with patients. How often have we heard the justifiable complaint: "The doctor never even touched me." Examinations allow for close union resulting in a proper diagnosis. A brash young surgeon I know brags that his philosophy of patient care is: "Meet them, treat them, street them." This may be modern medicine's view, but it leads to treatment errors, patient dissatisfaction, and higher insurance rates.

To fill the patient visit with discussion of laboratory results is also not enough. Doctors do not treat tests; they treat people. Teaching hands-on medical skills and patient-doctor relationships was once part of medical school curricula. These are no longer subjects and patients suffer from their absence.

Patients also complain that doctors no longer take the upper hand in decision-making. While it is important for patients to participate in treatment choices, the dialogue is blurred by physicians who agree with anything the patient wants in order to avoid possibilities of litigation. Patients are confused by their role in deciding courses of treatment or tests. The avalanche of medical information in the media makes people aware of treatment options. That's a good thing. Then, when the physician does not suggest possible tests or treatment, the patient feels obliged to offer the suggestion. A typical conversation: "Doctor, do you think I should have an MRI to see what this back pain is about?" Doctor responds, "If you want we can arrange that." That leaves the patient confused and feeling hypochrondriacal.

Advances in medicine today go beyond the wildest imaginations of physicians four decades ago. Saving and prolonging lives are modern achievements that cannot be ignored, but neither can the maintenance of the *art* and humanity of medicine.

As I look back over the two years I practiced in eastern Kentucky and compare it to the years that followed, I am struck by how much I grew. The foolish fears I had of snakes, rats, and creepy crawlers now seem insignificant. The fear of dead bodies is anathema to this aging physician, now amused by its revelation. My experiences with the Kentucky mountaineers left me fulfilled and satisfied, their stories and lives now part of my own. I earned their respect even as they helped abate my insecurities and inadequacies in the field of medicine, and in the game of life itself.

In eastern Kentucky I learned that "caring" for patients had a double meaning and that each was equally important. I also came away with the knowledge that the "care" went both ways.

EPILOGUE

When I left eastern Kentucky I knew I could not start practice in a big city. I finally felt ready for my own private practice, but did not want to become lost in a metropolis. Woodbury Heights, New Jersey was nothing like Kentucky, but it had the small town atmosphere I had grown fond of, and a nearby hospital was reminiscent of the quality of care of Miners' Memorial Hospital. I spent the remainder of a happy professional life in this New Jersey town, enjoying a status of a country doctor, but the changes that occurred in my last year of practice were difficult to live through.

The saddest change in modern medicine is the demise of the old family physician's home-based practice. My grand old Victorian house, a three-story behemoth on an acre of well-groomed lawn, was once my home and medical practice.

The first level, complete with lovely stained-glass windows, housed the office. Throughout my 37 years of practice, a full-time office assistant was my only employee. By keeping the practice small, I was able to assume traditional nurse's duties myself. I administered all injections and medications, discussed dietary management, insulin therapy, care of wounds, and all other problems that were, I believed the responsibility of the private family physician. This took time, but there was no rush, as the waiting room was not bulging with weary patients completing endless forms that invaded their personal financial lives.

Victorian chestnut beams, which covered the ceiling of the waiting room, sheltered a place for social interchange among patients. Personal art works or photographs from my travels were interspersed with displays of patients' own art creations on the walls. Price tags on the paintings benefited the artists, and the changing displays pleased and amused the patients.

My office assistant, Eleanor, worked with me almost from the start. She knew the patients personally and put their medical needs ahead of their insurance carriers or their financial positions, gaining patients' confidence because of her intimate relationship with them. An astute listener, she knew enough so that when a patient revealed a nonmedical problem that might relate to his or her physical condition, the information was passed on to me. Can you imagine a patient in today's medical complexes discussing anything other than insurance or payment information with the office personnel?

I lived on the second floor of the building while the third floor housed my art studio. It was here that I produced the stained-glass windows that added to the charm of the house. Patients knew that they could still get help by ringing the doorbell on the private residence side of the house in an emergency.

House calls were never refused and my frequent transportation was my motorcycle. Homebound patients were amused by the appearance of the "White Tornado," the name, lifted from a contemporary cleaning solution advertisement, was used by some of my hospital associates to describe me when I whisked around town on my motorcycle. Police contacted me for help in finding my patient Willie, the local drunk, who regularly ran the streets while nude. My car would find its way through the dark back streets, following the scent of boiled garbage to the heart of the pig farming area where Willie lived. I never found him on his naked jaunts, but these memories brought to mind the time he called me to come quickly because his wife was dying. The mournful laments of assembled family and friends, who assumed she was dead, were reaching a peak when I injected intravenous dextrose solution to bring her out of obvious insulin shock. "Praise the Lord; it's a miracle. The doctor raised her from the dead!" It was moments like this that produced a glow that made the practice of medicine seem worthwhile. The closeness I shared with Willie and his wife, Ella, however, came to a shattering end a few years later when his drunkenness drove him to psychosis. This time when I came to his aid I found Ella with a hatchet buried in her head. Willie, although temporarily insane, was convincingly sorry for having killed his wife. He spent the rest of his days in prison where, many years later, I eventually pronounced him dead of natural causes.

My 37-year practice in a small suburb of southern New Jersey was enhanced by this very personal involvement with my patients. Anecdotes about patients over the years kept my sense of humor alive. A 99-year-old devout Catholic hospitalized with an irregular heart rate was told she had to be converted in order to reestablish a normal cardiac rhythm. "Oh, no, doctor. I've been a Catholic all my life; you can't convert me now!"

Illiterate Jim was having the wax syringed from his right ear while I joked that we were in trouble if water came out his left ear. "Eh, what would that mean, doc?"

Meg, owner of a pig farm, took exception to a neighbor's complaints of the farm odors. "Where would you get bacon without us?" she declared. "In the supermarket, of course," retorted the neighbor.

On a sadder note was the patient who refused treatment and hospitalization for severe depression. Hours of talk with her and family members failed to convince her. As the decision for involuntary commitment was made, she was found dead by hanging in the garage. I am still awakened by the horror of the scene, and still wonder what I could have done better to prevent it.

As managed care invaded my limited private practice, the logistics of competing to stay in medicine became impractical. A large medical practice was never my goal. I enjoyed having time to spend with patients, and I enjoyed having more free time for myself. A large practice would have negated both. I decided not to do this because participating in a managed care program necessitated hiring two other employees to do all the added paperwork the system required. To pay for more help meant accepting new patients, destroying the type of practice I built.

I finally sold my practice to the community hospital, and a family practice resident was placed in the office part of the house, while a huge family practice center was built in a nearby town. Under the new management, the patient load dropped precipitously while the staff increased to three employees, plus a "practice management team" in control of all operations and billing. Office hours were theoretically expanded, but the doctor was available less and less of the time. Ordering drugs, vaccines and other supplies, preparing the rooms and sterilizing instruments were totally removed from a doctor's supervision. All bills were paid by the hospital through the professional manager.

The walls were stripped of any personal objects and replaced by notices naming various acceptable HMOs. Pictures of the new modern medical center that would soon replace the present building were substituted for patients' artwork. Clipboards with sign-in forms and elaborate information statements

kept patients busy while a new, confused staff super-
seded my knowledgeable single assistant. Patients
told me they missed Eleanor's friendly smile, and
her personal involvement in their health care.

I have to wonder why Americans allowed such
drastic changes in a system that once touted the
highest quality of medical care in the world. And
why did the members of the medical profession
allow themselves to become swallowed by the
morass of forms, paper work, diagnostic numbers,
and impersonal patient contact that medicine had
become?

The new staff finally moved to their elegant
quarters in a nearby town. What remains is a sad but
beautiful house that no longer meets the needs of a
modern medical office. No doctor today is interested in a home-based office practice. Walls that once
heard sad stories as well as laughter echo from lone-
liness. The house is cold, empty, and unwanted,
another casualty of managed health care.

ABOUT THE AUTHOR

Rita A. Mariotti graduated from The University of Pennsylvania in 1952 as an English Literature major and went on to earn a Medical Degree from The Woman's Medical College of Pennsylvania in 1957. "Coal Miners' Doctor," her first book since retiring from a 40-year career as a family physician in Woodbury Heights, NJ, is a memoir of the first two years of medical practice in eastern Kentucky as a coal miners' doctor. She is presently at work on a novel, also set in Appalachia, as well as a collection of poetry and haiku. Her work has appeared in *The New York Times, The Philadelphia Inquirer, The Star Ledger, Now and Then Magazine, The Pennsylvania Gazette, Medical Economics, Cuizine Magazine,* and others. She lives in Glendora, NJ, summers in Sea Isle City, NJ, and travels extensively.